SPIKE IT!

The #1 Sports Writer for Kids

MATT CHRISTOPHER

SPIKE IT!

Little, Brown and Company
Boston   New York   London

First Edition

The characters and events portrayed in this book are fictitious. Any sim-
ilarity to real persons, living or dead, is coincidental and not intended by
the author.

Library of Congress Cataloging-in-Publication Data

Christopher, Matt.
    Spike it! / Matt Christopher. — 1st ed.
        p.   cm.
    Summary: Unhappy at having to share space and family with her
new stepsister Michaela when her father remarries, thirteen-year-old
Jamie is further dismayed when Michaela joins her volleyball team
and becomes a star player.
    ISBN 0-316-13451-1 (hardcover). — ISBN 0-316-13401-5 (pbk.)
    [1. Stepfamilies — Fiction.   2. Remarriage — Fiction.
3. Volleyball — Fiction.]   I. Title.
PZ7.C458Sop   1999
[Fic] — dc21   98-46399

10 9 8 7 6 5 4 3 2 1

MV-NY

Printed in the United States of America

To Nicole

SPIKE IT!

1

ee-fense! Dee-fense!"

Jamie Bonner looked up at the bleachers running along the sides of the gym. The crowd was rocking the house, cheering for the opposing team. Jamie wiped the sweat from her brow with her wristband so she could get a better look at them.

The crowd was getting desperate, she realized. Pretty soon, if she had anything to do with it, this gym would be as quiet as a tomb.

Jamie's team, the visiting East Side Middle School Sharks, had already won the first game of the volley-ball match, 15–13. Now they were up, 12–10, over the Gaston Torpedoes in the second game of the best-of-three match.

Three more points, and another Sharks win would be in the books. Another step on the way to the

1

statewide middle school play-offs. Jamie tried to catch her breath as she rotated to the front row left position — hitter.

Hitter, that was her. That was the role that suited Jamie best. The attacker. The shark. Go for the kill and spike it down their throats!

She was definitely the most sharklike of the Sharks, although, at five feet six inches, she wasn't the tallest girl on the team. That distinction went to Jamie's best friend, Laurie Gates, who was now about to serve. Laurie was five nine, with blond hair tucked back into a ponytail. Her blue eyes danced among a million freckles.

There was a gentleness in those eyes that Jamie loved. Sometimes she wished she were more like Laurie, but she couldn't change who she was, could she? Ah, well. In some other ways, she realized, Laurie probably wished she could be more like Jamie. After all, that's how it was with best friends, wasn't it?

Laurie and Jamie looked like complete opposites — Jamie had dark hair, fair skin, and dark brown eyes — but they'd been inseparable since kindergarten. Jamie's dad sometimes called them "the mismatched bookends."

The ref's whistle blew, and time was back in. Jamie watched as Laurie tossed the ball up and served overhand — a line drive that barely cleared the net.

Jamie turned to face the play, watching as the receivers for Gaston got the ball to the setter, who hit it up to the front line — the hitters.

"Spike it!" Jamie heard the crowd shouting.

The girl opposite Jamie leaped into the air, let out a bloodcurdling yell, and reared back to smash the ball home. But Jamie was ready for her. At the last moment, she sprang into the air and blocked the spike!

As Jamie came down to earth, she could see the Gaston players diving to keep the ball alive. But it was no use. She had placed it perfectly. The ball skidded off to the side and hit the ground. The Gaston crowd groaned, and the Sharks let out a whoop.

"What a block!" Keisha Morgan shouted, giving Jamie a slap on the back. "You're bad, Bonner!"

Jamie gave her teammate a high five, then quickly turned her attention back to the game.

Jamie needed to keep her focus now. It wasn't easy. All day long, her mind had strayed back to the disturbing phone call from her dad.

3

Jamie looked up and saw Laurie glancing at her. *She can read me like a book,* Jamie thought, catching the look of concern on her best friend's face. *She knows I'm just barely holding it together.* Then it was back to the game, and the moment had passed.

Laurie's next serve was underhand, a high lob that caught the tense Gaston players off guard. Two of the girls in the back row went for the ball at the last instant, confused as to whose play it was. They just managed to get the ball to the front row, and the setter had to lurch to reach it. The best the hitter could do was a weak shot to the Sharks' back row. Keisha received it easily, and Laurie set up Jamie perfectly.

Jamie leaped up as the ball came to her, swung her right arm around in a windmill, and smashed it with all her might. The shot knocked one of the Gaston players to the gym floor, and the ball flew off into the disappointed crowd.

"One more!" Coach Molly McKean yelled, clapping her hands. "One more!"

The ball came back to Laurie and she served again, a line drive this time, to the far right corner. The receiver sent it high into the air, and the girl in front of Jamie spiked the ball right at her head!

Before Jamie could react, the ball was past her, just missing her head and landing out of bounds by inches! The crowd groaned in unison, and the Sharks mobbed each other in triumph.

But Jamie held back, shaken for the moment. That ball should have been hers. She could have blocked it. She had let her attention wander for one split second, and it had almost cost her team big-time. If the spike hadn't missed its mark, Jamie's mistake would have cost her team the serve — and maybe the victory.

On the court, the other girls were celebrating. "Nine and three!" Kim Park yelled, pumping her fists in the air. "Yes!"

"Still in first place!" Brittany Hernandez said with a big grin that showed her braces. "Look out, West Side, here we come!"

High fives were exchanged all around, and then the girls went over to shake the hands of the defeated Gaston team. Afterward, in the locker room, they gathered around Coach McKean, as they did at the end of every game, win or lose.

"All right, Sharks," the coach said, her penetrating ice blue eyes taking them all in. "We played our game today, and that's why we won. But as you know, the toughest part of the season is still ahead of us — including West Side Middle. They're nine and three, just like us, and only one of us is going to make the state play-offs. So enjoy this one, but stay hungry. Keep up the seamless teamwork, keep setting each other up and staying in position, and we'll be okay. Now, let's get cleaned up. The bus is waiting."

With one more cheer, the girls all moved off to their lockers.

As she showered and changed, Jamie felt herself getting all worked up again. She knew she was probably letting her imagination run away with her, but she couldn't stop thinking about that phone call from her dad last night. He'd said he had some big news to share when he returned.

He'd sounded happy — too happy. Jamie had a feeling she wasn't going to like what he had to say. As far as she was concerned, no news was good news. Her life was okay just as it was. She didn't need — or want — anything to change.

On the bus ride back to Milford, Jamie kept silent while the other girls whooped it up, laughing and kidding each other as they always did after a big victory.

Jamie caught Laurie eyeing her a couple of times, but she avoided her friend's glance. She didn't want to talk about what was bothering her. Not in front of all the others, anyway. Laurie seemed to understand, and didn't come over and sit next to her.

The bus dropped all the girls off in front of East Side Middle School, and Jamie and Laurie began walking the six blocks to Laurie's house. Since Jamie's dad had been in New York on business all week, she and her little sister, Donna, had been staying with Laurie's family.

"Okay, Jame. What's up?" Laurie finally asked her.

"Nothing, really," Jamie said.

"Sure. Right. Come on, this is me, remember?"

Laurie was like a twin sister to her, Jamie reflected. Ever since the day eight years ago when Jamie's mom died, the Gateses had been like a second family.

It had happened so suddenly — sick one night, an ambulance rushing her to the hospital, but the next day, Mom was . . . gone. Forever. Donna had been just a baby then. But Jamie had been old enough to remember her mom's face, and precious moments together. Jamie kept a few treasured photos of her mother in a leather envelope in her top drawer. Some nights, she looked at them before she went to bed.

The Gates family had been lifesavers back then. Even now, whenever Chuck Bonner had to go away on business, his girls always made their way over to Chester Avenue.

It was fun staying at the Gateses', Jamie thought with a smile. Donna was best friends with Laurie's little sister, Samantha, so neither Bonner sister felt lonely. The two fifth graders hung out together, leaving eighth graders Laurie and Jamie pretty much to themselves.

And then, of course, there was Jeff.

Jeff Gates was Laurie's *real* twin. He had the same blond hair as all of the Gateses, and he was tall, like both his sisters, but without Laurie's and Samantha's freckles.

Jamie had known Jeff for years, of course. But lately, every time she saw him she would feel herself blushing, and her heart would start pounding. Once or twice she had even dreamed about him.

It was the one secret Jamie had never shared with Laurie — and never would.

"So come on, what's bothering you?" Laurie asked. "Even during the match you were thinking about it. Not that it hurt your game much."

Jamie sighed. "Oh, all right — it's my dad. When he called last night, he was *unusually* happy — and something he said just got under my skin."

"Oh, really? What did he say?"

"Only that he had something really important to tell us," Jamie said. "The last time he said that was when my mom died."

Laurie blinked. "Yeah, but if he's happy, it must be something good."

"Good for *him,* maybe," Jamie said. "You know why he went to New York?"

"On business, right?"

"Yeah, but there's this lady who lives there. Tracy Gordon. I think I told you about her."

"She works for the same company, right?"

"Right, that's her. My dad met her at a company picnic in June, and Donna and I could tell right away that he had a crush on her. She's really

9

beautiful, with this dark red hair down to her shoulders. . . . And every time he goes to New York or she comes here, they see each other."

"And now, he calls and says he has big news. I see. . . ." Laurie nodded.

"Nothing against Tracy. I've met her a couple of times, and she's nice and all," Jamie said quickly. "It's just that — I'm so afraid he's going to marry her and we're going to have to move to New York!"

"Oh, Jamie!" Laurie dropped her book bag and gave Jamie a big hug. "You're getting yourself all upset, and it's probably nothing! Why don't you wait till you hear what your dad's got to say?"

"I just can't help it," Jamie moaned. "I'm so afraid something will come along and change my whole life. I don't want things to change!"

"Everything changes," Laurie pointed out.

"I know, but you know what I mean," Jamie insisted. "I've finally got to the point where I like things the way they are, even without my mom. . . ." She fell silent, blinking back tears.

"Look, promise me you'll just relax until you know more," Laurie said. "Why should you upset yourself in advance? Come on, at least wait till your dad gets home."

"Okay," Jamie said, sniffing and wiping her eyes. They were almost at the house, and she certainly didn't want Jeff to see her like this.

Donna and Samantha were riding bikes on the sidewalk, screaming their heads off and having a great time. When the ten-year-olds saw them approaching, they rode over.

"Did you win?" Donna asked, looking at Jamie expectantly. Donna had big blue eyes, just like their mom's. Jamie wished she had eyes like those.

"Yeah, we won," she answered. "Two games to zip."

"Was it close?"

"Not now, okay? I'll tell you about it later," Jamie said, heading for the front door.

"What's the matter, did you mess up?" Donna called after her.

Jamie rolled her eyes, shook her head, and kept on walking.

"I'll bet you messed up. Otherwise you wouldn't be so crabby."

"I'm not crabby!" Jamie shouted back. She didn't

turn to look at Donna. She just yanked the door open, and she and Laurie went inside. "Ugh. Little sisters can be such a pain!"

"Tell me about it," Laurie agreed with a laugh.

"Samantha's all right," Jamie said. "You don't know how lucky you are. You didn't get stuck with Donna."

"Oh, come on, Donna's not so bad," Laurie insisted. "She worships you, you know."

"Yeah, right!" Jamie said sarcastically. "That'll be the day."

"You just don't see it because she tries to hide it," Laurie said. "She can't fool me, though. Did you see the way she looked at you with those big blue eyes of hers? You're her idol."

"Her idol? Give me a break! Have you had your head examined lately?" Jamie couldn't help smiling. "Come on, it smells like your folks have dinner ready. I don't know about you, but I'm starved!"

Jamie noticed as they headed for the dining room that she was feeling a little better. She shook her head and laughed. "Idol . . . Yeah, right."

2

All through dinner, Jamie kept staring at Jeff. She knew she was doing it, but she just couldn't stop herself. Everything he said was so funny, or so true, or so perfect somehow.

Once or twice, he'd caught her looking at him and smiled, with that crooked grin of his she'd tried unsuccessfully to imitate in the mirror. Jamie had quickly looked away. She didn't want him to see her all red in the face.

After dinner, Jeff went out to play basketball with some friends from down the block. With him gone, Jamie's thoughts went back to her dad and the "big news" he'd promised to share.

While Laurie watched her favorite show on TV, Jamie packed her bags and brought them to the front door. Then she sat out on the stoop, waiting for her dad to come, getting more anxious with every passing moment.

Finally, after what seemed like years, the familiar green minivan came around the corner and pulled over at the curb.

Just then, Donna came running out the front door, flew right past Jamie, and threw herself into their father's arms. "Daddy!" she screamed.

"Donna! How's my baby?" he said, picking her up and spinning her around in the air.

Jamie came over and gave him a hug from behind the clinging Donna. "Hi, Dad. Welcome home."

"Hi, pumpkin!" he said, greeting her with a glowing smile that was almost overflowing with happiness. "Let's go thank the Gateses and get on home. I can't wait to tell you everything!"

On the way home, he wasted no time breaking the news. "Girls," he said, "do you remember Tracy, the nice lady I introduced you to at the picnic?"

Uh-oh, Jamie thought, swallowing hard. *Here it comes.*

"I like her, Daddy," Donna said. "She's nice."

"Well, I'm glad you think so, honey, because Tracy's going to be your stepmom."

Jamie stifled the groan that tried to escape from her throat.

"You're getting married?" Donna gasped. "Awesome! Can I be the maid of honor?"

"How about the ring bearer?" he suggested. "Would you like that?"

"Yesss!" Donna said, pumping her fist happily.

Jamie bit her lip. "I'm so happy for you, Daddy," she said, leaning over to give him a kiss on the cheek as he drove.

"I hope you're happy for you, too, pumpkin," he replied. "Just think — we'll be a complete family again after all these years!"

Jamie choked down a sob. Hadn't they *been* a complete family all this time, even without Mom? Did he think he could just bring this Tracy person in to replace her? And what was Jamie supposed to do? Forget all about her real mother?

The car pulled into the driveway. This was the house Jamie had always lived in. *Mom's* home. How could they just sell it and go somewhere else?

Trying to control the trembling in her voice, she asked, "If you get married, do we have to move?"

"Why no, pumpkin," he said reassuringly, "we're going to stay right here in Milford."

Jamie felt an enormous weight slip off her shoulders. As long as she didn't have to leave Milford, she thought, she could put up with almost anything.

But what her father said next took Jamie completely by surprise.

"I know the house is a bit small for five, but we'll make do somehow."

"Five? Don't you mean four?" Jamie asked.

"Well, the three of us, plus Tracy, and her daughter, Michaela. Didn't I tell you about her?"

No, of course you didn't! Jamie thought, suddenly furious. *Daughter? What daughter?*

"You mean I get to have a new sister?" Donna asked excitedly. "Cool! How old?"

"Thirteen, and she's a peach," their dad said happily. "Yep. We're going to be one big, happy family!"

Jamie felt a wave of dizziness wash over her. "There are only three bedrooms, Dad," she pointed out. "How are we all going to fit?"

"Well, we'll have to see," he replied. "For the mo-

16

ment, Michaela can use the convertible sofa in the living room. Once their stuff gets here, we'll have to shift things around a bit."

Jamie kept silent as her dad unloaded their bags. She stood there, too stunned to move.

"I'm sorry to spring this on you girls so suddenly," he said, seeming to sense what Jamie was feeling. "I would have loved to let everybody get to know each other first. But Tracy works in New York, and we weren't totally sure this was going to happen until she got her promotion last week. She's moving to our local branch here — we're going to be working in the very same office, isn't that great?"

He put an arm around each of his daughters' shoulders and hugged them tight. "I love you both so much," he said in a near whisper. "We'll make it work. It'll be great — you'll see."

"I want to hear all about Michelle," Donna said.

"It's Michaela, honey," he corrected her. "And you'll get to know her soon enough. She and Tracy are moving in day after tomorrow!"

"*What?!*" Jamie blurted out before she could stop herself. "Isn't that kind of soon?"

"Well, the wedding is set for Saturday, so —"

"Saturday?!"

Donna was jumping up and down. "Yay, a wedding! I can't wait to greet my new mom and sister! Can I make a cake for them, Daddy?"

Their dad laughed. His brows unfurrowed and he seemed to relax. "Sure, baby, that would be fantastic. Er, maybe you could get Jamie to help you?"

That made Jamie mad. How could he just volunteer her like that? She didn't want to bake a cake for people she barely even knew — and she wasn't sure she wanted to live with them, either!

"I don't want Jamie to help me; I want to do it myself!" Donna insisted.

"Fine. For once we agree. Do it yourself," Jamie said, fighting back tears as she ran into the house.

She still couldn't believe her dad had acted so rashly. How could he have sprung this on them? Did he have any idea what he was doing?

Incredibly, Donna didn't seem at all bothered. Bringing total strangers into her home was just fine with her.

Donna was too young to remember, Jamie reminded herself. The image of her mother's face flickered in her mind for a moment, then faded.

She never really knew her. Of course she doesn't remember.

Her dad now came into the house, carrying all their bags and whistling a snappy little tune. Donna skipped in after him.

They seemed so happy! Jamie shook her head in disbelief. What planet were they on, anyway?

Not the same one she was, that was for sure.

3

"They're here! Jamie! They're here!"

Two beeps of the horn told the girls their dad was back from the airport with Tracy and Michaela. D day had arrived.

As Donna ran eagerly out the front door, Jamie lagged behind. A sudden sense of dread came over her. Lifting the living room curtain, she peeked through the window, watching as everyone else hugged and kissed each other.

Jamie had met Tracy a couple times before, of course. The first thing she'd noticed was how tall and beautiful Tracy was. Even Jamie's mom hadn't been *that* pretty. *No wonder Dad fell in love again,* she thought with a frown.

Now she focused on Michaela for the first time. Michaela looked a lot like Tracy — tall, red haired, pretty, athletic looking — but with a certain added impishness in her features that Tracy didn't have.

Jamie forced herself to calm down. The last thing she wanted to do was ruin everyone else's happiness. She went slowly outside, bracing herself.

"Jamie! Come on over and say hi!" her dad called to her.

Jamie could hear the worry in his voice. He hadn't forgotten her reaction the other night when he'd announced his wedding plans.

Jamie went up to Tracy and gave her a little peck on the cheek. "Hi, Tracy. Welcome. Congratulations."

"Oh, Jamie," Tracy said, gazing back at her with a glowing smile, "this is such a big moment in all our lives. I'm so thrilled this has happened. I can't wait to get to know you better!"

Jamie pasted a smile onto her face. "Yeah. Me, too," she said quickly.

Obviously her dad must have said something to Tracy. Something like "Jamie's taking it badly. Better be extra nice to her."

Jamie turned to Michaela before the phony smile faded from her face. "Hi, I'm Jamie," she said, and stuck her hand out stiffly.

"Michaela. Hi." Michaela took Jamie's hand and shook it. She didn't smile, but looked questioningly into Jamie's eyes, seeming to ask, "Is it okay with you that we're here?"

Ugh! He's told Michaela, too! Jamie broke free and looked away as quickly as she could. She was so glad neither of them had tried to hug her. That would have been too much to bear.

"I hope all this didn't come as too much of a shock to you," Tracy said, putting a hand on Jamie's shoulder.

"No, not at all!" Jamie lied.

"I know it must be hard —"

"No problem." Jamie cut her off. Then, luckily, she spied a way out. "Uh, here, let me help with your bags."

Jamie knew she had to keep busy doing a million things, or else she might let her real feelings show. No, she decided, crying would definitely not be cool right now.

But why couldn't her dad have taken more time to prepare her for this? Why did he have to just spring it on them all of a sudden?

She knew she couldn't stop what was happening. Tracy and Michaela were not going to disappear tomorrow, no matter what Jamie did. She knew that resenting them was unreasonable. After all, they seemed nice enough. They hadn't done anything bad to her.

Oh, well, Jamie thought. *Who knows? Maybe I could actually get used to having them here — if I can just get through tonight!*

For the next half hour, while the grown-ups did some unpacking, the three girls sat around the kitchen table, getting acquainted over ice cream.

It had been Donna's idea, and Michaela had eagerly taken her up on it. Now the two of them were giggling as they drizzled chocolate syrup over their banana splits.

Jamie played with her one scoop of plain vanilla, taking an occasional spoonful into her mouth. She wasn't hungry. In fact, she was on the edge of nausea.

Not that the other two noticed. Donna was oblivious, totally entranced by Michaela. And if Michaela sensed that Jamie was unhappy, she was doing a really good job of hiding it.

Right from the first, Donna had been so busy

trying to impress Michaela that Jamie couldn't get a word in edgewise. Even worse, Michaela had seemed totally interested! She laughed and nodded at all Donna's stupid fifth-grade jokes and gossip. It was like being with two fifth graders!

Jamie just sat there, trying not to barf. Either Michaela really liked hanging out with little kids or she was humoring Donna — in which case she was a really good actress. Jamie wasn't sure which was worse.

That evening, they all went out to a restaurant for dinner. There, to Jamie's continued annoyance, Donna kept showing off, not even caring that she was in public.

"Wanna see my monkey face?" she asked Michaela. "It's really cool!"

And Michaela laughed at the stupid face as if it were the funniest thing in the world. Jamie had seen the monkey face a million times. It hadn't been funny the first time.

Worse, her dad didn't even try to shut Donna up! He just sat there, smiling like a goon, and so did Tracy.

"Please, I'm trying to eat," Jamie commented when Donna did her *Phantom of the Opera* face.

Donna frowned. "Cheer up, Jamie," she said. "Michaela's not being crabby, and she had to come all the way from New York and lose all her friends and stuff."

"Shut up, Donna!" Jamie hissed. "I'm not acting crabby. You're acting like a jerk." She glanced quickly at Michaela, who seemed taken aback by her sudden outburst.

"Now, kids!" Suddenly her dad looked worried. "We're in a restaurant. Try and get along, will you? Unless you can think of something nice to say, don't say anything!"

"Sorry," Jamie muttered, glaring at Donna.

"I can say something nice," Donna offered. "I think Michaela is really nice. A whole lot nicer than —"

"Donna! Stop it this instant!"

Jamie could see that her dad was angry. Oh, well. At least he was madder at Donna than at her. That little brat deserved whatever she got, for sucking up to Michaela so much.

And to think, Laurie had said just the other day that Jamie was Donna's idol. Jamie had almost believed it then. Well, so much for that. Donna had a new idol now.

4

The wedding took place as planned on Saturday. With so little advance notice, only a couple of dozen people had been invited. But since the ceremony took place in the gazebo in Milford Park, there were lots of onlookers, passersby who stopped to witness the event.

Everyone seemed touched by how affectionate the bride and groom were. Even Jamie felt her eyes welling up with tears. It was great that her dad was so happy. For years after her mom's death, Jamie would hear him every once in a while, crying through the closed door of his room. She would go in and comfort him, and they would hug, just the two of them missing her, neither one of them ever saying a word.

Yes, it was good that her dad was happy now. But

there would be no more wordless moments like the ones they'd shared.

Jamie had worn her best dress for the wedding — the flower print she'd worn to the seventh-grade end-of-year dance. She wanted to look good when she gave her father away. From the proud, tender way he looked at her before he took Tracy's hand, Jamie knew she'd succeeded.

Michaela was the bridesmaid, and Jamie had to admit she looked gorgeous in the off-the-shoulder green dress she'd borrowed from her mother.

Donna made the most of her role as ring bearer, and everyone in the crowd commented admiringly on her big blue eyes and angel face. Even Jamie took pride in how cute her little sister was. But when the ceremony started, Donna held Michaela's hand, not hers. That really stung Jamie. She had to gulp back the tears.

During the wedding vows, Jamie got all choked up again, along with everybody else. Her dad had lost his wife to a sudden illness. Tracy, she knew, had lost her husband to a drunk driver. It was a second chance at love for both of them.

Then the preacher cleared his throat. "If anyone

present knows why this man and this woman should not be joined in holy matrimony, let them speak now, or forever hold their peace."

Jamie bit down hard on her lip, stifling the words that threatened to escape.

"You may kiss the bride," said the preacher. And everyone cheered. Jamie sniffed back tears and tried to smile.

Afterward, there was a raucous party at a local restaurant. There hadn't been time to hire a band, but Freddie McIntyre, the local DJ, was a friend of Chuck Bonner's, and he came with his whole setup and played a mix of dance music.

Everyone was dancing. Jamie's dad was kind of comical, the way he moved, but Tracy was really good. She and Michaela got up and danced together, and it was the highlight of the whole party. Michaela was an even better dancer than Tracy. She had a natural grace about her that Jamie envied.

Jamie wondered if the two of them would ever be friends. It was beginning to seem possible to her, this idea of having a new, bigger family.

Laurie and Jeff Gates were dancing with each

other. Jamie would have given a lot to switch places with Laurie right at that moment.

"Wanna dance with your old dad, pumpkin?" Jamie turned around to see her father smiling at her, his hands held out for hers.

"Sure," she said, and let him lead her around the floor to a corny old Frank Sinatra number.

"How're you doing?" he whispered in her ear as they swayed back and forth.

"Pretty good. You and Tracy looked so perfect together," she told him. "It was a beautiful ceremony."

"I'm glad," he said. "And how do you like Michaela?"

"She seems okay," Jamie admitted. "Maybe I could get to know her better if Donna would leave her alone for a minute. It's so annoying the way she acts."

"She's just trying to make a new friend," her dad assured her. "Donna still loves you best, you know."

"Yeah?" Jamie replied, unconvinced.

"Come on, pumpkin," her dad said, giving her a little squeeze. "I can see you're worried about it, but believe me, it's just the fascination of someone new. Donna'll settle back down to normal after a while."

"I sure hope so," Jamie confessed.

"Besides, you and Michaela are the same age. You're going to be together a lot at school. You'll soon find out you have lots in common."

"Mmm."

"Trust me. She's a great kid, you'll see."

"Okay, Daddy."

Then he cleared his throat. "And you know, Jamie," he said tentatively, "as you said yourself, the house is pretty small for five people. We're all going to have to share space. Me with Tracy, you with Michaela . . ."

"What?"

Jamie caught her breath. She broke free and stared at her dad. "What are you talking about? I thought she was sleeping on the sofa in the living room!"

"For a couple of days, yes . . . but once her bed arrives —"

"Where is all *my* stuff supposed to fit?"

"Shhh!" Her father glanced around to see if anyone had heard her complaint. "Look," he said in her ear as the music played, "we'll work it out eventually, Jamie. But until we save enough money to add on to the house, or move to a bigger place, you're going to have to share your room with Michaela."

"But —"

"Jamie . . ." His tone had a stern warning in it. "Not here at the party. Please. This isn't the time or place."

Jamie stood there on the dance floor, frozen. She felt like she was losing her father, her little sister, and now her bedroom, all at the same time! Pretty soon she'd have nothing left — nothing that was all her own.

5

That night, her dad came to tuck her in. "Feeling better?" he asked.

"Dad," Jamie said in a hoarse whisper so no one outside the room could hear. "This is so unfair! Why do I have to share my bedroom? It's my own private place! Can't we fix up the basement for her or something?"

"The basement isn't exactly a nice place to sleep," he said. "How would you like to sleep down there?"

"I'd rather do that than share this room," she lied. There were spiders in the basement. Creepy, crawly spiders, and who knew what else?

"Come on, you don't really mean that, Jamie. It's just for a while — six months to a year, maybe. We'll start looking for houses in the spring, or add on to this one, okay?"

"A year's a long time, Daddy!" Jamie complained.

"I'm sorry, pumpkin. But we can't always get everything we want when we want it, you know?"

Uh-oh, she thought. *Here comes one of Dad's "little talks."*

"I think it's time we had a little talk, young lady."

Young lady. She loved that. And why was it that during their "little talks," he did all the talking?

"Look, I want you to understand something, Jamie. This isn't easy for Michaela, either. She's just left her school, her house, all her friends behind. She's coming into a strange new situation. It's a much harder adjustment for her than it is for you. I should think you'd want to give her a helping hand."

Jamie sat silently. What was there to say? She guessed she was just a bad, selfish person. But she couldn't help how she felt, could she?

"Now, I expect you to behave like a good stepsister and help make Michaela's adjustment go smoothly."

"Fine," Jamie said through clenched teeth. "But I'm keeping my stuff right where it is," she said, trying to salvage something from the wreckage of her life. "She'll have to find space to put her things, because I'm not moving mine. I mean, nobody's helping me with *my* adjustment."

"I'll help, pumpkin." Her dad knew he had won the battle, and he could afford to be generous in victory. "I'm glad we had this little talk," he said, kissing her on the forehead. "You'll see, honey. You're not losing your room. You're gaining a new friend."

Jamie rolled over to face the wall. At least it was better than facing reality.

She didn't know when she'd fallen asleep, but when Jamie woke up, the house was still dead quiet. It was eight o'clock on a Sunday morning, and everyone was still worn out from partying the day before. Everyone but Jamie.

She went downstairs and tiptoed through the living room so as not to wake Michaela, who was sleeping on the sofa. She glided silently into the kitchen and had some cereal for breakfast.

Looking around as she ate, Jamie felt as if the house itself had suddenly turned against her. There was no one here she could talk to, no one who understood what she was feeling. In fact, if they knew how she really felt, they'd hate her for it, she was sure.

Jamie thought of calling Laurie but realized it was too early and she'd wind up waking the Gateses. It was only Laurie she wanted to speak to; only Laurie would understand.

She finished eating, went upstairs, and got dressed. Today was the last day she could call her room her own, she reflected. Tomorrow, it would be Michaela's, too.

She looked around at her posters on the wall, her trophies and treasures displayed on the bookcases, her stuffed animals, the painting she'd done in fourth grade. *Oh, well,* she thought. *Michaela will just have to deal with it. She can keep her stuff in the attic until she gets her own bedroom.*

An hour later, Jamie and Laurie were in the Gateses' backyard, popping a volleyball over a net to each other. In between hits, Jamie poured out her heart to her friend. Laurie took her time thinking over what Jamie had said.

"I don't know, Jame," she finally said. "It doesn't

seem like the end of the world to me. Like I said, change happens. Nothing stays the same forever. And it could have been worse, right? No matter what, you're not leaving Milford."

"That's true," Jamie said. She tossed the ball in the air above her. As it fell back to earth, she linked her hands and held her arms ramrod straight out in front of her. Using the underside of her forearms, she sent the ball back over the net to Laurie.

Hands above her head, Laurie used her fingertips to gently return the ball.

"Besides," Laurie continued, "Michaela seems really nice. Maybe she'll turn into a friend if you give her a chance."

Jamie gave the ball a ferocious dig with one arm. The ball ricocheted off the net and fell to the ground.

"She'll never be my sister, I'll tell you that," Jamie blurted out. "I've already got one of those, and it's one too many."

"You don't really mean that, and you know it," Laurie said, coming under the net to put an arm around Jamie's shoulders. "You know, it's good Donna and Michaela get along so well. Think what would happen if they didn't!"

Jamie couldn't help smiling. "Donna would make everybody's life miserable," she said, imagining the horror of it. "Have you ever seen one of her tantrums?"

They both laughed at that one. But Jamie quickly lapsed back into her funk. She still didn't like the way Donna and Michaela had taken to each other so fast.

The girls lobbed the ball back and forth in silence for a while. Then Laurie spoke.

"Jame, there's no going back," Laurie said simply. "You just have to accept it and make the best of it. And as for sharing your room, I think you should be patient. It's just for a while, right?"

"A year is longer than 'just a while,'" Jamie said miserably.

"Well, I guess you could share your room with Donna instead. . . ." Laurie said.

"What? No way!" Jamie said, horrified. "She's a total slob and ugh — yuck! How could you even suggest it?"

The two girls laughed. "I guess it is a rotten idea," Laurie admitted. "Besides, it would make Michaela feel isolated in her new family, and that wouldn't be good."

"Mmm. I guess I could make more of an effort to be nice to her," Jamie said. "I could help her get used to school tomorrow — you know, introduce her to everyone and stuff."

"Looks like she's already making friends," Laurie commented, looking down the driveway.

Jamie followed Laurie's gaze, and her breath caught in her throat. There, at the head of the driveway, stood Michaela, talking with Jeff! The two of them were standing only inches apart, talking and laughing, looking into each other's eyes. Jeff had his hands in his pockets and was kind of rocking back and forth with a goofy smile on his face.

Jamie felt the blood rush to her cheeks. Her heart was hammering so loudly she was sure Laurie could hear it.

"Gee," Laurie said with a mischievous grin, "looks like Jeff has a crush on somebody, huh?"

Jamie tried to answer, but the words wouldn't come out. She swallowed hard, blinking back tears. It felt like she was drowning.

Michaela giggled at something Jeff was telling her. Then the two of them started walking toward the house.

"Oooh, I can't wait to give him the business about it," Laurie was saying.

"Yeah," Jamie managed to agree. It was a good thing Laurie wasn't looking at her or she'd guess the truth in an instant. "I've got to use the bathroom," Jamie said quickly. She tossed the ball to Laurie, hoping her friend wouldn't see her expression.

She locked herself in the bathroom, splashed some cold water over her face, and stood there leaning over the sink until her heartbeat and breathing returned to something like normal. *Talk about total disaster!*

Maybe Laurie was right. Maybe Michaela was the nicest girl in the universe. But one thing was for sure. Whether by accident or on purpose, she was moving in on everything Jamie wanted her to stay away from!

I'm so glad we have two classes together," Michaela said as she and Jamie walked the six blocks to school. "I'd feel totally lost otherwise." She took her program card out of her book bag.

"Well, I may not be that much help," Jamie said truthfully. "Math and history aren't exactly my strongest subjects."

"Really? What classes do you like?"

"Science is my favorite," Jamie said. "That's probably because Mr. Klimik teaches it. He's a really good teacher, and by the way, he's also gorgeous."

"And I didn't get him?" Michaela let out a mock groan. "Let's see . . . Ms. Grimaldi. How's she?"

"Everyone says she's good," Jamie said. "And you'll like Ms. Cook, our history teacher. She's nice, although I never seem to get all the dates and facts straight. I guess I'm just not that into it."

"How's Mr. Marra?" Michaela asked.

"Yuck." Jamie made a face. "He used to teach college, and he thinks we're all math geniuses. Nobody's running better than a B in his class."

"Hmm . . ." Michaela frowned. "I hope I'm not going to be too far behind. I've already missed almost a week of school since we left New York."

"You'll be okay," Jamie assured her. "We're all in the same boat in math."

She and Michaela had been getting along pretty well so far. Jamie hadn't let on that she'd seen Michaela with Jeff, and Michaela hadn't talked about him either, except to say how nice the Gates family was.

Donna was still making a fuss over Michaela, but Jamie had gotten used to it, at least for the moment. Her dad had said it would all blow over in time. For now, Jamie was willing to believe him.

Jamie also figured she could at least make an effort to be friends by helping Michaela out on her first day at East Side Middle. It was a place she knew inside and out after more than two years here.

And because she was a star of the volleyball team, Jamie was also one of the more popular girls in the eighth grade. She guessed the least she could do was to introduce Michaela to everyone so she wouldn't start life here as a total stranger.

Jamie saw a bunch of her friends now, standing outside the school waiting for the bell to ring. Her Shark teammates Kim Park, Megan Hicks, and Brittany Hernandez were there. So was Tina Macaluso, the captain of the cheerleading squad.

"Hi, Jamie!" Kim called out with a wave. "Practice today after school."

"I know," Jamie answered. "Hey, you guys, I want you to meet Michaela Gordon. She's my new stepsister."

"Michaela? Cool name!" Megan said, shaking hands.

"Really?" Michaela asked, obviously pleased. "I don't know, everyone's always misspelling it."

"Well, I think it's unique. Hi, I'm Megan. I'm in seventh grade, but they let me hang out with them anyway." Everyone laughed, and the other girls quickly introduced themselves. "Wow, I love your hair!" Tina said. "Do you curl it?"

"Uh-uh," Michaela replied. "It just does that. I can't make it straighten out."

"Why would you want to?" Brittany asked with a giggle. "It's awesome."

"Hey, do you play sports?" Megan asked.

"Sure!" Michaela said. "I'm into all kinds of things — sports, music, dancing, acting . . ."

"Guys . . ." Kim added jokingly, and everyone cracked up.

Just then the bell rang. "Uh-oh, we'd better go in," Tina said. "Who do you have first period, Michaela?"

"Um, let's see . . . English. Room 202. Ms. O'Brien."

"Hey, me, too!" Tina took Michaela by the elbow. "Come on, I'll show you where it is."

"See you later, everybody," Michaela said with a wave. "Thanks, Jamie! See you in math class?"

"Yup. See you."

Jamie watched Michaela and Tina walk down the hall, deep in animated conversation.

"Lucky you, Jamie," Kim said.

"Your new stepsister's great!" Megan commented.

Well, she sure isn't shy, anyway, Jamie thought.

43

In fact, Michaela seemed to have the knack of charming everybody she met.

"Now, who can tell me the value for X in this equation if X is a natural number and b equals a?"

Jamie felt her brain squeezing like a sponge, trying to even comprehend what Mr. Marra was talking about. As usual, he was teaching his class as if his students were all Ph.D.'s.

Jamie shot Michaela a look that said "See what I mean?" To her amazement, Michaela actually had her hand up!

"Yes, Michaela?" Mr. Marra said.

"X equals three a plus twelve b," she said.

"Correct!" Mr. Marra seemed dumbfounded that one of his students actually knew the answer. "Michaela, that's very, very good! This is not an easy equation. Here, let's try another one."

The entire class sat amazed as Michaela answered the next equation, and the next, and the next, sometimes without even using pencil and paper.

After the bell rang, Michaela was surrounded by several other students, all of them wanting to know how she figured out all those impossible equations.

Great, Jamie thought. *She's a brain, too. Just what I need. Somebody who's prettier, smarter, and nicer than me, and lives in my room.*

By the time Jamie arrived at the cafeteria for her lunch period, she was beginning to feel miserable again. She searched for Michaela, since they'd agreed to meet here and talk about how the day was going.

At first Jamie didn't see Michaela. But that was because she was looking for a tall, redheaded girl standing or sitting by herself. Then Jamie noticed a large group of boys gathered around a table at the far end of the cafeteria. They were surrounding someone who was almost totally hidden from view. Then the circle parted to reveal Michaela, who was obviously thrilled to be the focus of all that attention.

Jamie came closer, and now she could see that all the boys seemed to be competing to be the funniest or the coolest. And worst of all, sitting right next to Michaela was none other than Jeff Gates!

"Hi, Jamie!" Michaela called out, motioning her to come over. "Here. I saved you a seat."

"Hi!" Jamie said, making her way through the knot of boys who seemed totally unaware of her existence. "What's going on? I didn't know you were such a celebrity."

"Neither did I, believe me!" Michaela said with a happy laugh. "But I'm having a great time — this school is awesome!"

"You think so?" Jamie asked.

"Oh, yeah!" Michaela said. "The classes are fun, the teachers are nice, and I'm not behind at all, like I was afraid I would be. And best of all, everybody's being so friendly!"

Jamie shot a quick glance at Jeff, who was smiling dreamily at Michaela as if she were a movie star or something. "Listen," Jamie said, "I'm not really that hungry. I think I'm going to go do some studying, okay?"

Michaela shrugged. "Sure, okay. Don't worry about me, I'm fine," she assured Jamie.

No duh! Jamie thought as she quickly made her way out of the cafeteria. She hurried to the nearest girls' room and locked herself into one of the stalls.

She sat there for the next fifteen minutes, trying to compose herself so that no one in her afternoon classes would know that her entire world was falling apart.

46

7

Jamie managed to get through the rest of the school day without any further damage to her psyche. Volleyball practice provided a needed relief. She and Laurie, as usual, dominated the intrateam scrimmage.

On the volleyball court, at least, there was no question about who was on top. Here, Jamie's world was still her own. Her spikes were fearsome, her sets precise, and her serves a confusing mixture of high underhand lobs and powerful overhand smashes.

When practice ended, Jamie felt better than she had in a long time. She was almost disappointed when it was time to go.

Later on, when she got home, the moving van delivering Tracy and Michaela's stuff was just pulling away. Jamie went inside, where everyone was busy rearranging furniture. "Hi, all," she called out. "Gotta go do my homework, okay?"

"Go ahead, honey," her dad said. "We've got everything under control here. We put Michaela's bed in your room already, so everything's all set in there."

Alarmed, Jamie rushed upstairs to survey the damage to her room. Michaela's bed stood against the wall opposite hers. There were a few boxes of stuff on the bed, and the closet was pretty jammed with both girls' clothes. All in all, though, Jamie had to admit that it wasn't too bad. Her posters still covered the walls, her trophies were still on their shelves, her stuffed animals were still in their corner. It would be crowded, but at least the room looked pretty much the same.

Jamie sat down to do her homework and quickly bogged down over the math equations Mr. Marra had given them. She was still trying to figure out the first one when Michaela came into the room, sweaty and dirty from lifting boxes.

"Hi," she said, giving Jamie a big smile. "Whew. I've done about all I can do for one day. How's the math coming?"

"It's not," Jamie said, tapping her pencil on the page in frustration.

"Want me to go over it with you?" Michaela offered. "I've already finished the assignment."

Jamie gritted her teeth in a smile. "No, thanks," she said. "I'd rather figure it out for myself. I'm not a total idiot, you know."

"I never said you were," Michaela replied, then shrugged off Jamie's crabbiness. "Oh, well, suit yourself. I'm going to take a shower." She grabbed a towel and headed for the bathroom, then paused at the door. "By the way, thanks for today. It was awesome."

Jamie shrugged and shook her head. "I had nothing to do with it," she said sincerely. "You didn't need any help."

"You're wrong," Michaela told her. "I couldn't have done it without you. And if you want any help with math later, feel free to ask." With that, she disappeared down the hall.

Yeah, right. Like I'd ever ask you for help, Jamie thought bitterly. Her good mood from practice had vanished. She went back to her equations, but the numbers seemed to dance before her eyes. Finally, she threw down the pencil in frustration and got up out of her chair. She hated math! Hated it!

Then she saw Michaela's books strewn across her unmade bed. Curious, she wandered across the room and peeked at Michaela's notebook. All the equations were written out neatly. There was no crossing out where she'd made mistakes. Everything had been done right the first time. Jamie seethed with jealousy.

She shut the notebook, but she now knew the answer to the first equation. It had been right there in front of her, impossible to ignore, although she hadn't really meant to see it.

Jamie went back to her desk and tried to copy out the formula from memory, but about halfway through, she faltered and had to go back for another look. "Oh, well," she muttered. "What does he expect, when he gives such hard homework?"

Knowing Michaela would be out of the shower in a few minutes, Jamie did something she'd never done before in her entire life. She grabbed Michaela's notebook and hurriedly copied down the equations and their answers. Then she put it back exactly where she'd found it. Jamie glanced around guiltily, then went downstairs, feeling lower than a worm.

"Jamie?" Michaela's voice was soft in the darkness.

"Yeah?" Jamie's grip on the sheets tightened, and her breathing sounded loud in her ears. Was Michaela going to accuse her of stealing the math answers? Had she found Jamie out?

"I was just wondering. . . . Do the girls on the volleyball team ever play just for fun? You know, like a pickup game?"

Jamie's initial reaction was relief. Her cheating had gone undiscovered, it seemed. Then panic began to set in. Michaela had already moved in on her life in every conceivable area, with the single exception of volleyball. Jamie was determined not to let her last preserve be invaded.

"Oh, sometimes, I guess. When the season's over," she said tentatively.

"Really?" Michaela sounded disappointed. "Never before?"

"No, not usually." Jamie was beginning to sweat. She didn't like where this conversation was going.

She let out a loud yawn to signify that she was tired and didn't want to talk about it anymore.

"Oh! Am I keeping you up? I'm sorry," Michaela said immediately.

"It's okay. . . . It's just . . ." Another yawn. "Just that we've got a big game tomorrow, and it's late. . . ."

"A big game? Who are you playing?"

Jamie cursed herself for saying too much. Now Michaela was back into it again. "Kingsboro Middle," she said, trying to sound totally exhausted. "They're pretty good. Only a game behind us in the standings."

"What place are you in?" Michaela wanted to know.

"Tied for first with West Side. Nine wins, three losses. Only one team from our division makes the statewide play-offs."

"Wow! So this really *is* a big game," Michaela said. "I guess I should let you sleep."

"Mmmm," Jamie agreed, pretending to already be drifting off.

"How many games in the season?" Michaela asked.

"Fifteen."

"Oh — so it's almost over." There was a note of hurt in Michaela's voice.

"Pretty much. But you can always take up volleyball in high school. It's never too late."

"Of course, if you make the play-offs, which you'll probably do, there'll be lots more games, right?"

Jamie scowled. She didn't like where this was going one bit. "Uh, right."

"Hmm." Jamie could hear Michaela sitting up in bed. "It's just that, well, I played volleyball last summer, and people told me I was pretty good. It wasn't organized or anything, and I'm not sure we were even playing by the rules, but it was a lot of fun. That's why I was hoping you guys played pickup games sometimes. So that maybe I could play . . . or maybe even join the team. Do you think?"

Jamie's heart started hammering. "I have to say, I doubt you could jump in in the middle of the season," she said discouragingly. "It would take something pretty major for Coach McKean to add a new player when the team's already complete."

"Oh," Michaela said, sounding disappointed. "I

was only asking because . . . well, because since you're on the team, I thought it would be cool if I tried out, and we would be teammates."

"Yeah, well . . . maybe you could get on the basketball team," Jamie suggested. "Their season is just starting, and they aren't that good. They could probably use somebody tall who can play the game. You play basketball, don't you?"

"I did in New York," Michaela said. "I kind of liked volleyball better, though."

"Oh?" Jamie sat straight up in bed.

"Yeah," Michaela shot back. "All I know is, it was a blast. Anyway, forget it. Whatever."

"Yeah, whatever." Jamie thought she detected a little annoyance in Michaela's tone. Had Michaela caught on to the fact that Jamie didn't want her on the team?

Jamie hoped so. She didn't mean to hurt Michaela's feelings or anything, but if that's what it took to keep her away from the Sharks, so be it.

"Well, g'night," Jamie said.

"Thanks again for today," Michaela said. "Jamie — you really think I did okay?"

"Are you kidding? *Everybody* liked you."

"Whew!" Michaela said, laughing in mock relief. "Yeah, I guess it went pretty well, huh? I was so scared this morning."

"Whatever," Jamie said again. "I'm really tired, Michaela. Talk to you in the morning, okay?"

"Oh, okay. Sorry. I know you need your sleep. And, um, what time is the game tomorrow?"

"Four o'clock," Jamie said.

Oh, no! Jamie thought. *Is she going to show up at the game now? Great, just great.*

Jamie knew Jeff Gates was going to be there, and she'd been looking forward to impressing him with her play on the court. Now he'd probably be talking to Michaela the whole time, not even watching the game.

"Four o'clock? Oh, no!" Michaela said. "That's when Drama Club tryouts are. They're doing *Brigadoon* this year!"

"Oh, gee, that's too bad," Jamie said, relieved. "I guess you'll miss the game, then. Oh, well, there'll be at least two more games after that, even if we don't win the division."

"Mmm . . ." Michaela's tone told Jamie that she was thinking hard. But about *what?*

"Drama Club is excellent," Jamie told her. "They do great stuff. You'll love it."

"Mmmm . . ."

Jamie smiled and pulled the covers up to her chin. *Think all you want,* she said to herself. *That audition will take hours. And as for joining the team, forget it. Not in this lifetime!*

8

I got it!" Jamie screamed, and dove for the ball. Inches from the ground, she got her hands under it and hit it high in the air, setting up the hitter perfectly. Seconds later, the Sharks notched another point.

"'Atta girl, Jamie!" Coach McKean shouted. "What a play! Let's get 'em, Sharks!"

The two teams had banged away at each other for over an hour, with the lead seesawing back and forth. The first game had gone to the Kingsboro Mustangs, 15–13. In the second, the Sharks had built an early lead, then lost it, only to come back and win, 17–15.

Laurie and Jamie had been the stars of the match so far. Whenever either of them made a great play, the fans in the stands erupted — and leading the cheers was Jeff Gates.

Jamie glanced over at him now. He gave her a raised fist and a grin, saluting the incredible save she'd just made. Jamie felt her cheeks go red, but she gave him a smile before returning her attention to the game.

Jamie was having her best match of the season, and she knew it. Three times, when the Sharks had been on the verge of losing the second game, she'd made great plays to save the day.

It was now almost five-thirty, but the long match looked as if it was going to result in a big win for East Side Middle. They now led, 9–2, and had momentum going their way.

Keisha Morgan was serving. She was not normally a great server, but she had gotten into a groove, mixing crosscourt serves and lobs, keeping the Mustangs guessing and tentative. With her serving, the Sharks had scored nine points in a row.

But this time, Keisha's serve was short. The hitter on the other side of the net leaped up to spike it right back. Laurie, seeing the empty spot on the court, dove under the ball and sent it back aloft.

Then Laurie hit the ground hard. She let out a cry of pain as the play went on. Jamie heard the cry and hesitated. But she knew Laurie would want her to keep the point going before helping her.

With Laurie down, the Sharks were a player short, and the Mustangs took full advantage, hitting the ball to spots where Laurie, slumped on the ground, was in the way of the other players. After a heroic effort on the part of the Sharks, the Mustangs won the point, and service went back to them.

Now everyone rushed to Laurie's side. She was sitting up, holding her wrist. "I just landed on it funny," she told the coach. "I'll be okay. Really."

"Never mind. You're coming out," Molly McKean said sternly. "Hicks, you're in." She lifted Laurie up and led her to the bench. "Let's get some ice and a bandage over here right away," she told one of the bench players.

The whistle blew, and play resumed. Jamie worked harder than ever now, and no points were scored for the next five minutes as the momentum shifted back and forth.

It was Jamie's turn to serve now. She held the ball in her left palm and was about to hit it, when she saw the gym doors swing open and Michaela walk in.

Michaela saw Jamie staring at her and waved.

Then she turned to find Jeff in the stands. He waved to her with a big grin on his face and indicated that she should come sit next to him.

"Come on, Jamie, let's go!" Kim Park said. "What are you waiting for?"

Jamie frowned and hit the serve. Perhaps because she was distracted, the serve went off line and landed out of bounds. The crowd groaned. Jamie looked up to see Michaela and Jeff sitting together, talking a mile a minute. *Good,* she thought. Maybe they hadn't seen.

But from that point on, Jamie began blowing shots left and right. She was continually one step too late, or caught off guard, or missing easy hits.

"Come on, team!" Molly McKean shouted. "What's going on? Let's get with it!"

Jamie blushed, knowing "team" meant her. She was messing up royally, and with everyone watching, including Jeff!

She cursed under her breath. Michaela was ruining her concentration!

Bam! The ball hit her hard, before she even saw it. It ricocheted away before she could react, and another point was scored for the Mustangs, who had now retaken the lead, 10–9.

"Bonner!" Coach McKean called out. "Sit down. Hernandez, you're in."

Jamie smashed the heels of her hands together in disgust as she headed for the bench. She couldn't believe it — the game was on the line, and the coach was taking her out! It had never happened before, never come close to happening.

Jamie sat next to Laurie and shook her head in disbelief.

"I'm sorry," Laurie said softly. "We were doing great till I tripped over myself like a klutz."

"You made a great play," Jamie assured her. "I'm the one who messed up." She gave Laurie a hug just as the Mustangs scored yet another point. With Jamie and Laurie both out, the visiting team was pressing its advantage.

"Coach, put me back in!" Jamie begged.

Molly McKean frowned, then nodded. After the Mustangs won the next point, she reinserted Jamie into the game, this time in the front line.

The score was 14–12, Mustangs. Match point, and

the visitors were serving. It was now or never for the Sharks, and Jamie geared herself for one final effort. The play began and turned into a long volley, with tremendous saves and hits on both sides. Jamie waited for the ball to come to her, ready with every fiber of her being.

Then her glance strayed, for one split second, to the stands. Michaela was sitting only inches away from Jeff. They were watching the game intently — and Michaela had her hand on Jeff's!

"Spike it!" someone yelled.

Jamie looked up to see a tall Mustang hitter towering over the net. She tried to react, but the ball hit off her upturned palms and skittered out of bounds.

The match was over. The Sharks had lost.

And it was all her fault!

The disappointed Sharks stood on the court, dazed in defeat, as the Mustangs mobbed each other.

Laurie came up to Jamie, still holding her injured wrist. "Good try, Jame," she said weakly.

"Yeah, great. I messed up totally," Jamie said, feeling the words catch in her throat.

"Nah," Laurie said, throwing her good arm

around her. "It was my stupid wrist. If I'd been in there, we would have pulled it out."

"You okay?" Jamie asked.

"I think so," Laurie said. "It hurts, but not too bad."

They headed for the locker room. Jamie cast one last glance over her shoulder at the stands, but Michaela and Jeff were nowhere to be seen.

Jamie let her tears mingle with the water from the shower coursing down her cheeks. She'd cost the team a crucial victory, in front of the home crowd, with Jeff in the stands watching the whole thing.

And it was all Michaela's fault!

When Jamie got home, she smelled something delicious emanating from the kitchen. It surprised her, because she distinctly remembered her dad saying he and Tracy had to work late tonight — some big meeting they were preparing for.

Had the meeting been canceled? She went into the kitchen to find out — and stood motionless at the door.

There, standing in front of the stove, tending to two simmering pots of food, was Michaela! Donna sat at the table, watching admiringly as her new stepsister cooked up whatever it was that smelled so good.

"Hi, Jamie!" Michaela greeted her cheerfully, as if nothing had happened.

"Hi," Jamie said warily, then slowly approached the stove. "What are you doing?"

"She's cooking, dummy," Donna said with a giggle. "What's it look like?"

Jamie gave her a poisonous look. "I can see that, thank you."

"It's jambalaya, with sautéed veggies," Michaela explained. "I thought I'd surprise Mom and Dad when they come home."

Mom and Dad? She'd called them "Mom and Dad"! So. Michaela now thought of Jamie's father as her dad! Well, Jamie was never going to call Tracy "Mom." Never in a million years.

"Too bad about the game," Michaela said in a sympathetic tone that Jamie found really annoying. "But Jeff says you guys still might make the play-offs."

"Yeah, well, whatever," Jamie replied, not wanting to talk about either the game or Jeff.

"He was telling me all about the rules and stuff," Michaela continued. "How the receivers have to hit it to the setters, and they hit it to the hitters. It's more complicated than I thought."

"Yeah. I told you it wasn't easy to learn," Jamie agreed. "Did you audition for the Drama Club?"

"Yeah! I got in, too!" Michaela said. "Mr. Fishman said I have a natural talent for acting."

Jamie frowned. She had to agree on that one. Michaela had everyone thinking she was so nice, while all the time, inch by inch, she was taking over Jamie's life.

Jamie knew that by cooking dinner for everyone, Michaela was just trying to outdo her. Jamie could not remember the last time she herself had cooked anything.

"Hey, how's Laurie's wrist?" Michaela asked.

"She thinks it's okay," Jamie told her.

"Oh, good. Jeff was worried about her."

"Jeff likes Michaela!" Donna piped up in her most annoying tone.

"Oh, stop it, Donna," Michaela said, blushing.

"Yeah, stop it," Jamie agreed in a menacing voice.

"It's true, and you know it," Donna insisted, giving Michaela a mischievous look. "And you like him back."

"I do not!" Michaela waved a spatula at Donna, but she couldn't help smiling. "Now cut it out! You're embarrassing me. Here. Come here and help me stir this."

"Okay." Obediently, Donna went to the stove and busied herself with the food.

Jamie's eyes wandered around the room and came to rest on something she hadn't noticed before — a yummy-looking cake with chocolate icing and multi-colored roses. "Where'd you buy the cake?" she asked, going over to it.

"Michaela *made* that!" Donna blurted out. "And she showed me how to do the icing, too — I did the flowers all by myself!"

Jamie was stunned. "When did you find time to do all this stuff?" she asked Michaela.

"Oh, I started the cake last night, and the rest of the dishes I just sort of improvised from what I found in the freezer and the pantry."

"Huh. Well."

Jamie didn't know what to say. She was floored, and she knew her dad and Tracy would be, too. Well, she guessed that was what came from having a mom when you were a kid. A mom who could teach you how to cook and sew and all that stuff. Michaela was lucky. Luckier than she was, anyhow.

"Okay, everything's just about ready. Go set the table, okay?" Michaela asked Donna.

"Yes, sir!" Donna saluted and ran to get the cloth napkins and the good silverware.

"Well, I guess I'll go do my homework," Jamie said. "Looks like everything's under control here without me."

As she went into the living room and sat down on the couch to sift through her schoolbooks, Jamie felt her lower lip trembling. She bit down on it hard.

Dad and Tracy would be home any minute. She sure didn't want to spoil everybody else's party. Why shouldn't they be happy? Just because *she* was miserable?

"Oh, Michaela, this is absolutely divine! You've outdone yourself!" Tracy raved, rolling her eyes in delight as she tasted the jambalaya.

"It was nothing," Michaela protested modestly. "I had a good helper." She indicated Donna, who blushed with pride and pleasure.

"I hope you're taking notes, Donna," Chuck Bonner said. "If you can learn to cook like this . . . Wow! Michaela, I had no idea you were so talented — and in so many areas, too! That's really great about the Drama Club!"

"Thanks," Michaela said, smiling. "I'm totally psyched about it."

There was silence for a few seconds. Then Donna said, "Jamie's team lost the big game."

"Thanks a lot, Donna," Jamie muttered quickly.

"Oh, I'm sorry to hear that," Tracy said.

"Too bad," her dad said, shaking his head. "What happened? Did you guys have a bad day?"

"You might say that," Jamie said, looking away. "Um, I'm not very hungry. May I be excused?"

"But you've hardly eaten anything!" her dad objected. "And it's so delicious. Besides, Michaela worked so hard to make it."

"I'll eat it later, maybe," Jamie said. "Now, can I please go upstairs? I'm not feeling too well."

"Oh," her dad said, giving her a long look. "Why didn't you say so in the first place?"

"Would you like me to bring you up some tea or something?" Tracy asked.

"No, thanks," Jamie said. "It's nothing, really." She got up quickly and left the dining room. One more second of Michaela's triumph and her own disgrace and she would have burst into tears right there in front of everyone.

Jamie slowly climbed the stairs to her room and opened the door.

"What the —?!"

Jamie could not believe her eyes. Her room had been totally transformed. Instead of her posters, hanging on the walls were totally different ones — everything from movie stars to female athletes to rock bands.

Michaela! Somehow, in the time it had taken Jamie to get home from the game, Michaela had managed not only to get dinner cooking, but to steal Jamie's room as well!

Jamie felt something snap inside. Suddenly, it was as though she were standing outside her own body.

She heard herself shouting, saw herself ripping down the posters and tossing them onto the floor, felt the hot tears streaming down her cheeks.

By the time she heard the footsteps running up the stairs, the walls were bare, and the floor was littered with the torn remains of Michaela's posters.

Michaela appeared in the doorway and let out a horrified scream. "Jamie!" she yelled. "Look what you did to my posters!" She flew at Jamie, her fists flailing, and the two girls went down in a heap on the bed.

Jamie curled up into a defensive posture, just trying to fend off Michaela's assault. Michaela was still screaming and grabbing fistfuls of Jamie's hair to pull.

Then Jamie kicked hard, knocking Michaela off her. Before she could recover, Jamie leaped on top of her and tried to pin her down.

"Hey! Hey! What's going on here? Jamie, get off her! Stop it this instant!"

Jamie heard her father and Tracy shouting at them, but both girls resisted being pried apart. At last, the adults succeeded in separating them. They stood panting, staring at each other with murder in their eyes, as their parents held them back. Donna stood in the doorway looking frightened, her big eyes even wider than usual.

"She ripped down all my posters!" Michaela shouted, pointing an accusing finger at Jamie.

"You took all mine down first!" Jamie shot back. "Who told you you could do that without my permission?"

Jamie's dad cleared his throat. "Um, actually, I did," he said. "It's my fault. I told Michaela she could put up some of her own posters if it would make her feel more at home."

"In *my room?*" Jamie howled. "Didn't it occur to you to ask me first?"

"I . . . I just thought it would be all right with you," her dad said.

"Well, it isn't! I don't want her stuff in my room, and I don't want *her* in here either!"

"Jamie!" Her dad looked horrified. "You don't mean that."

"Yes, I do!" Jamie shrieked. "I didn't ask for her to come live here! When did I get to vote on it? Nobody even asked my opinion!"

Michaela let out a sob, and Tracy cradled her in her arms to comfort her.

Jamie broke free from her father and stared at him defiantly.

He stared right back at her, and his lips were tight with anger now. "Jamie, I'm surprised and disappointed in you. You can just stay up here for the rest of the evening and do without dessert. And while you're at it, clean everything up. I expect you to replace all these posters out of your own money and apologize to Michaela for the horrible things you said."

"She hates me," Michaela whimpered into her

mother's shoulder. "Why does she hate me? What did I ever do to her?"

"You can share my room with me," Donna said, going over to Michaela and taking her hand. She stared at Jamie with a look Jamie had never seen before. It was a mixture of surprise, disappointment, and disgust.

"Jamie's just being a jerk," Donna told Michaela. "I used to think she was nice, but she isn't. She's mean."

"That's enough, Donna," Chuck Bonner said to his daughter. "Come on, everyone. Let's go back downstairs. I don't want this to ruin our evening — any more than it has already. Jamie's got some growing up to do, and she's got to do it by herself."

They all left the room. Tracy was the last to go. As she softly closed the door, she gave Jamie a look of sympathy mixed with genuine sadness. "I'm so sorry you feel this way," she said in a voice that was almost a whisper. "I hope you'll change your mind in time."

The door closed with a soft click. Jamie buried her head in her pillow and sobbed, crying out for her mother, who would never come back again.

10

When Jamie awoke the next morning, she was alone in her room. That much, at least, she'd achieved. Of course, it had come at great expense. But at least Michaela was out of Jamie's space. She'd spent the night on the living room sofa. Tonight her bed would be moved into Donna's room.

Jamie wasn't exactly proud of the way she'd acted, and when she thought of the money, time, and energy it would take to replace Michaela's stupid posters, she felt like kicking herself.

She dragged herself out of bed and left for school without sitting down for breakfast. She didn't want to have to talk to anyone. Not that they tried talking to her. In fact, they barely looked at her. Mutual silent treatment was the best anyone could manage right now.

Jamie thought that at this point, everything that could have gone wrong already had. But she soon found out she was mistaken.

When she got to school, Laurie was standing at the front gate, the center of a tight knot of very upset looking Sharks.

Her wrist was in a cast!

"Oh, no!" Jamie groaned. "Laurie, it's broken?"

Laurie shook her head but didn't smile. "Just a sprain. But I can't play for at least two weeks."

Jamie gasped as the other girls looked on in mute despair. "But that's the whole rest of the regular season!"

"I know," Laurie said. "But look at the bright side. It could have been worse — a break or something. As it is, I think I'll be okay for the play-offs."

"The play-offs?" Jamie repeated in disbelief. "How are we supposed to make the play-offs without you?"

"You've got to!" Laurie cried, looking around at all of them. "You've just got to!"

"Look, these things happen," Coach McKean said at practice that afternoon, her face a mask of concern.

"We'll just have to find a way to win without Laurie. Because I'll tell you one thing. If we don't win our next two games — including the one against West Side — I don't think we'll make the play-offs. West Side is not going to lie down and die so that we can win the division. We're all going to have to step up now, understand?"

"Yeah!" everyone shouted, responding to the urgent tone in their coach's voice.

"All right, now let's get up and scrimmage."

The Sharks divided into two teams of six each, with Coach McKean filling in for Laurie. Jamie was on the opposite team. She and Laurie had always done that, the two best players splitting up to make it fair.

Jamie could see that Coach McKean was holding back from the action, trying to see which of the Shark substitutes would be able to replace Laurie in the starting lineup.

Though all the girls were capable players, not one of the substitutes showed the energy or ability Laurie had. It wasn't their fault — for some of them, it was their first year on the team.

After practice, Coach McKean gathered them all together by the bleachers. She looked them all over.

"Okay. Good practice. I can see we're not just going to fold up down the stretch. But I can't help wishing we had a full roster to go into these last two games."

The girls all exchanged glances. What was Coach getting at? Jamie wondered.

"I don't want to do anything that would upset our team chemistry," the coach continued. "East Side Middle's not that big a school, and everyone who wanted to be on the team came down to tryouts in September.

"At that time, I took everyone I thought could help us be a winning team. But I don't know, maybe I missed someone. Does any of you know of anyone who might be able to help? Maybe someone who didn't try out but who wants to now, and is a good athlete?"

Michaela's voice popped into Jamie's head. *". . . since you're on the team, I thought it would be cool if I tried out."*

Jamie ignored the voice. She kept her mouth shut and looked from girl to girl to see if anyone else could think of someone. No one did. Jamie breathed a sigh of relief.

At that very moment, as if on cue, as if she'd been

listening at the door the whole time, just waiting to make her big entrance, Michaela burst into the gym. "Hi!" she called out, then stopped when she saw the team sitting in the bleachers. "Sorry. I didn't mean to —"

"No, not at all," Coach McKean assured her. "We're done. What can I do for you . . . ?"

"Michaela. Michaela Gordon. I'm Jamie Bonner's new stepsister."

"Oh, yes, I heard your name mentioned in the teacher's lounge," the coach said, shaking Michaela's hand and giving her a warm smile. "Mr. Marra says you're a math whiz. Anyway, welcome to East Side Middle." She gave Michaela an up-and-down look, and Jamie knew she was taking in her height and apparent grace in one glance. The coach cracked a smile. "Want to try out for the volleyball team, by any chance?"

Michaela blinked and smiled back. "Actually, it's funny you should ask," she said. "Because that's exactly why I came down here."

"Really? Wow, that's a coincidence."

"Not totally. I heard from Jeff Gates that Laurie couldn't play, so I thought you might have an opening." She turned to Jamie and gave her a satisfied smile.

Jamie gritted her teeth and shot back a sickly smile of her own.

"Well, can we give you a quick tryout?" the coach asked.

"Totally!" Michaela dropped her book bag and took off her windbreaker. Sure enough, she was wearing a T-shirt, gym shorts, and sneakers. "What do I do first? I have to warn you, I don't know much about volleyball."

"We'll take it easy on you at first," the coach promised. "All right, teams, form up again. Kim, place Michaela and make sure she knows what she's supposed to do."

Jamie stood there steaming while Kim led Michaela to the front line and explained what a hitter was supposed to do. Jamie placed herself directly opposite Michaela, so that they were facing each other across the net.

"Nice move," Jamie said under her breath so that only Michaela could hear her.

"What?" Michaela said, pretending she didn't understand.

Yeah, right, Jamie thought. *Little Miss Innocent. Like you have no idea what you're doing.*

The new scrimmage started. On the very first point, the ball came to Michaela. She jumped up, impossibly high, and spiked it so hard that no one came close to saving the point.

"Whoa! Did you see that?" Megan Hicks asked Jamie.

"Your new stepsister's awesome!" Keisha Morgan marveled.

"Maybe she just got lucky," Jamie said lamely.

Pretty soon, though, it was clear that luck had nothing to do with it. Michaela was a natural athlete; she was tall and had long arms, quick reactions, and a real feel for the game. Her serves weren't great, but her form was good, and anyone could see that she'd gain control of the serve, too, in time.

"You sure you haven't played much?" Coach McKean asked her, stepping out onto the court when the tryout was over.

"Well, I did play on a team last summer," Michaela admitted. "It wasn't anything organized, though, just a bunch of girls and boys getting together to play."

"Yeah, you looked really comfortable out there," the coach said, smiling. "Particularly as a hitter. I've never seen the ball spiked so hard."

"So," Michaela said, "do I make the team?"

"Sharks," the coach said, turning to the team, "I think we may have just found ourselves a new set of jaws."

Amid the cheers that filled the gymnasium as everyone mobbed Michaela, Jamie stood alone, rigid as a statue.

It was her worst nightmare come true!

11

That evening, Jamie lay in bed, staring out the open window at the rising full moon. The late October wind was blowing, and the papery leaves were swirling around. She could see them in the light of the street lamp, whirling in chaos. *Just like my life,* she thought.

In just a week, her whole world had been snatched from her grasp. Strangers lived in her house, her dad and little sister hated her, the guy she liked had a crush on her new stepsister, who, by the way, was suddenly the most popular girl at East Side Middle. And now Michaela was going to be a star player on the Sharks!

It's the final straw, Jamie thought. There was no way she and Michaela could ever be friends. Yet Jamie was going to have to live with her no matter how she felt! The grim future passed before her eyes — years and years of her and Michaela avoiding each other's gaze, not saying a word, pretending the other didn't exist. . . .

Donna would never forgive her, either. *Not that I even care. That little brat,* Jamie thought, blinking back tears.

The way her dad looked at her was the worst thing of all. Jamie knew she had ruined his chance at happiness forever.

She could feel everyone's gaze on her everywhere she went around the house. Even at school, she had gotten an occasional funny look from someone and wondered if that person had been talking to Michaela about her.

Jamie wished she could simply crawl away and disappear, but she just couldn't help the way she felt. The worst part was, even when no one was around, she couldn't escape her own judgment. To herself, she seemed small and petty, mean-spirited and jealous. She hated seeing herself that way, hated not being able to stop herself.

She looked at her alarm clock, the numbers glowing green in the dark room. It was only 9:45.

Jamie flicked on the bedside lamp. She looked up at her posters, back on the walls where they belonged. Yes, she'd won that battle, at least. Although it didn't make her feel any better, the bedroom was hers again. Hers alone. Dad and Tracy had moved Michaela's bed across the hall earlier in the evening.

Jamie got up to go to the bathroom. She could hear them all as she walked down the hall. They were downstairs in the living room, playing a board game, being a happy family. The tears welled again in Jamie's eyes.

Things just cannot go on like this, she thought. *Something's got to change, or I'm just going to explode.*

She locked the bathroom door and examined her face in the mirror. It was still the same Jamie — brown eyes, shoulder-length dark hair, long lashes . . . but something had changed. Something was subtly different about her features. Maybe it was that she hadn't smiled in so long. Or maybe she was just growing up. Almost fourteen . . .

The thought hit suddenly. Next week! Her birthday was next week and she'd totally forgotten!

Oh, well, there sure wasn't going to be any birthday party. No big celebration for Jamie. Who would come?

Donna probably wouldn't even bother to give Jamie birthday smacks like she usually did. You don't give birthday smacks to someone you despise.

Jamie washed her face and hands and went back to her bedroom. She didn't want a party, she decided. Better to let the day pass unnoticed. That was the way it was going to be anyway, so why wish for anything else? She'd be lucky if anyone even said "Happy birthday."

Lying in bed again, she thought of Laurie — her one true friend, the only person who still liked her for who she was. Suddenly, she had a tremendous urge to go see her.

But it was already after ten o'clock. Tomorrow morning, first thing, she'd catch up with Laurie and pour her heart out. Maybe Laurie could make some sense out of all that had happened. If she couldn't, Jamie thought, then nobody could.

Laurie was out front of the school the next morning, getting her cast signed by a bunch of her friends.

They were all laughing, kidding around. *Not a care in the world,* Jamie thought, sizing them up.

When she saw Jamie approaching, Laurie said something to the others, then separated herself from the group and came over to her. "Hey," she said. "What's up?"

"Nothing much. My life is over, that's all," Jamie said. "It's one humongous disaster, and I can't do a thing about it."

"Hmm," Laurie said. "Sounds like we need some time to talk. And the bell's about to ring. Can it wait till lunch?"

"Why not?" Jamie said with a shrug. "At this point what's the difference?"

"Oh, boy," Laurie said. "Michaela?"

"Michaela," Jamie said.

Just then, the bell rang and everyone headed for class. Jamie and Laurie joined the throng, Laurie leaving with a wave to go upstairs to science.

Jamie somehow managed to get through the morning, though she doubted she'd remember a thing that was taught when the time came for tests.

At lunchtime, she and Laurie got sandwiches instead of hot lunch. They went through the doors to the large outdoor courtyard behind the cafeteria. It was mostly cement, with some trees and grass here and there and a few cement benches. Laurie and Jamie found an empty seat and sat down.

"Okay, I'm listening," Laurie said.

"Oh, Laurie," Jamie groaned. "You're the only one I can talk to. Everyone else hates my guts!"

"Come on, now, I'm sure that's not true," Laurie began.

But Jamie cut her off. "Take my word for it, okay? I acted like a jerk, but trust me, I couldn't help it. Everybody loves Michaela — she's gorgeous, smart, nice, a good athlete. I'm sure she's telling all her hundreds of friends what a rotten person I am."

"*Are* you?" Laurie asked.

"What do you mean?"

"Just what I said," Laurie said. "Do *you* think you're a rotten person?"

"I told you, I acted like a jerk. I told Michaela in front of Dad, Donna, and Tracy that I wished she'd never come here. How's that for starters?"

"Whoa. Kind of 'out there,' I'd say," Laurie had to admit.

"You see? And I ripped her posters off my walls."

Laurie cleared her throat. "I have to tell you, I already heard about that one."

"From who?" Jamie blinked. "Samantha?"

"Jeff, actually," Laurie told her. "But Sam knew, too. You can't really expect Donna and Michaela not to talk about things like that."

"I guess not," Jamie said, sighing sadly. "So my reputation is ruined, right?"

"No, of course not," Laurie assured her. "It's never too late to turn things around."

"Yeah, right."

"Jamie . . ." Laurie gave her a stern look.

"It isn't?"

"Of course, you'll have to give it some time," Laurie added. "People's feelings don't heal just like that."

"But you don't understand," Jamie protested. "I really *don't* want her here! She moved right in on everything — even the volleyball team! She's a total manipulator! Doesn't anybody understand why I would hate her?"

"I do," Laurie said. "I understand, Jamie. But you've got to deal with it. I can see why you might feel she's been a little manipulative, but look at it from her point of view. If she just hangs back and doesn't push herself forward a little, she'd never get to know anybody. I admit she's not exactly shy —"

"Ha! You can say that again!"

"But you've got to give her a chance," Laurie finished. "Underneath that pushy exterior, she's a really nice girl. I've had a chance to get to know her myself — she's been over to see Jeff once or twice — and I like her."

"Oh. I see." Jamie felt as if she'd been punched in the stomach. "You too."

"It's nothing against you, Jamie!" Laurie said, putting a hand on hers. "It's just that you can't see the real Michaela because you're too upset. But unless you can let go of your attitude, and soon, you're going to do yourself and your family lasting damage."

Jamie swallowed hard. She stared at her tuna sandwich, not the least bit hungry. *Even her best friend liked Michaela better than her!*

"Look, Jamie, you've just got to give Michaela a chance. I know it must be hard for you, but it's —"

"Hard for her, too?" Jamie finished for her. "I know, I know. That's what everybody says."

"They're right, Jamie," Laurie said, gazing into

her eyes with a pleading look. "Trust me; Michaela's really okay — you'd like her if she weren't your stepsister — and the sooner you realize it, the better."

They heard the bell ringing for fifth period. Jamie stood up and tossed her half-eaten sandwich into the trash barrel. "Oh, well, I'll try," she promised. "Thanks anyway, Laurie. See you later."

"Jamie?" Laurie called after her. But Jamie didn't turn around. She headed for her next class, surrounded by a crowd of other students, feeling more alone than she'd ever felt in her life.

12

The next twenty-four hours passed without incident. No one in Jamie's family tried to reason with her. Michaela pretty much stayed out of her way, except to say "Please pass the salt" at dinner and stuff like that.

Of course, just because she and Michaela didn't fight didn't mean Jamie had a pleasant evening. Tomorrow was Mr. Marra's big math test, and Jamie hadn't paid any attention in class all week. Now she had to make up for lost time. Of course, Michaela, the math brain, didn't study at all. Instead, she spent some time helping Donna do her homework.

At one point, when Jamie came through the living room to get some lemonade out of the fridge, Michaela and Donna stopped talking until she was out of earshot. Jamie could easily imagine the kinds of things they'd been saying. And the worst part was, Donna knew all kinds of embarrassing stuff about her — and now Michaela would know it all, too.

Jamie snorted. What did she care? If they hated her, well, she hated them right back. She walked back through the living room with her lemonade, shooting them both a plastic smile. "Don't let me interrupt," she said cheerfully as she headed up the stairs.

Tomorrow was going to be a miserable day, she thought with a pang. Not only was Michaela going to breeze through the math test while she herself struggled, but tomorrow was also the first game the Sharks would play with Michaela on the team.

Jamie thought back — had it only been the other night? — to when Michaela had first asked her about playing volleyball. She'd said she didn't know the rules, Jamie remembered. But she wondered just how much Michaela really knew about the rules of the game — written and unwritten.

"Okay, Sharks." Coach McKean's eyes looked right at each of them like ice blue knives. "You know we badly need this match. As luck would have it, West Side lost their game yesterday, so our records are still tied. But remember, if we lose today, we put ourselves in a deep hole. Even if we win, we'll still have to beat West Side to get there. So everything is on the line today.

"I know this is a team we should handle pretty easily, but we can't take anything for granted. So don't be looking ahead to the West Side game. This game is our whole season. Now put your hands together."

The girls did their usual cheer, Michaela included. She was wearing Laurie's jersey, with the number one on the back of it. Laurie had explained to Jamie that there was no other way — it was too late in the season for Michaela to get her own uniform. But it still galled Jamie. Just another log on the fire that was burning inside her.

The Hillsdale Hornets had a record of 3–12 and were, by the look of them, not going to be a very tough opponent, especially since they were the visiting team. Jamie stretched her muscles in anticipation. This would be her chance to show Michaela how the game of volleyball was played.

The Hornets must have heard that there was a new player on the Sharks, because early in the match, they kept hitting the ball at Michaela. Unfortunately for them, the plan backfired big time. Every time the ball came to Michaela, even when she was in the backcourt, she sent it right back over the net at them, scoring points left and right.

After every winner she hit, the other girls whooped it up, delighted. "Yeah!" Keisha Morgan shouted. "We've got us a new ballplayer!"

Jamie shook her head in disbelief. The Sharks were all giving Michaela high fives, congratulating her, applauding all her ball hogging!

Jamie glanced over at Coach McKean. She had her arms crossed in front of her and wasn't saying anything, but Jamie could tell from the smile on her face that she wasn't exactly upset that Michaela was destroying all the teamwork Coach had worked so hard to teach them.

For sure, Jamie thought, *Coach will talk to her about passing the ball more during the next time-out.*

But no. When the next time-out was called, all Coach said was "You're doing fine, Michaela. Keep it up. Keep it up!" and patted her on the back.

Jamie hadn't seen much action, what with Michaela

taking nearly every shot. But now, when the team walked back onto the court leading the first game by a score of 11–3, Jamie was a stick of dynamite about to blow.

Michaela was serving, with Jamie in the front line directly in front of her. The serve was just so-so this time — the first one Michaela had launched that had been returned. As the ball came back over Jamie's head, she backed up to retrieve it, only to feel Michaela smashing into her from behind!

The ball hit the floor, and Jamie wheeled around to glare at Michaela.

Michaela stared right back at her. "That was supposed to be my shot," she said in a low voice that only Jamie could hear.

"Yeah. They're all your shot," Jamie muttered back.

"Bonner!" Coach McKean yelled. "Hold your position! Let the back row set you up!"

Jamie caught her breath. Coach had just criticized her in front of everybody! She hadn't done that all season. Jamie felt her face reddening. She bit down hard on her lip, humiliated, and turned back around to play the next point.

This time, she leaped up in time to make a tremendous, smashing spike.

"Ow!" the opposing player yelled as the ball glanced off her head.

Jamie smiled bitterly. "Yeah. Take that," she muttered, heading for the back row. It was her turn to serve, and she took the ball from Kim Park.

Michaela was still standing in the server's spot, waiting. *She's forgotten to rotate,* Jamie realized. Suddenly, a powerful impulse entered every fiber of her being: a strong, irresistible compulsion to give Michaela just a little, tiny taste of embarrassment. She heard Laurie's voice in her head, scolding her for even thinking about it, but Jamie shut it out. She didn't want to hear how nice Michaela was. Not ever again.

"Here you go," Jamie said, holding the ball out to Michaela. Michaela, unsuspecting, took the ball. Jamie looked away, as if she didn't even know what was happening.

Michaela launched the serve before any of her teammates had a chance to stop her. The referee blew her whistle. "Illegal serve!" she yelled, pointing to Michaela.

"What?!" Michaela gasped in horror. "Jamie —"

"It was my serve!" Jamie shot back. "Why'd you take the ball out of my hands?"

"You gave it to me!"

"I did not!"

"Hey!" Coach McKean shouted. "Michaela, keep your head in the game! Let's go! Time's in!"

The teams kept playing, and Jamie worked to conceal the smile that threatened to appear on her face. Coach had yelled at Michaela. Now the two of them were even.

She could feel Michaela's eyes burning a hole through her. Jamie didn't turn to her left to look, but she was pretty sure Michaela knew she'd done it on purpose.

Now it was Michaela's turn to steam. She threw herself into the game with a fury, banging point after point, until the first game was over and the Sharks had won, 15–3.

During the time-out between games, Jamie watched to see if Michaela would complain and was surprised when she didn't. She just sat there, letting herself be slapped on the back and congratulated by everyone. She looked at Jamie and smiled as if to say, "Living well is the best revenge."

That smile of hers drove Jamie crazy. *One way or another,* she swore to herself, *I'm going to wipe that smile off Michaela's face!*

The second game began with Jamie in the back row and Michaela in front of her. When the ball came to Jamie on the first pass, she passed it to Michaela — hard. Not only that, she delivered the pass to where Michaela couldn't hit it.

Jamie felt a surge of satisfaction as Michaela misplayed the ball. On the next point the same thing happened. Twice in a row, Jamie had actually succeeded in making Michaela look like a klutz.

The third time, Michaela finally blew. She jumped at Jamie, slapping at her and screaming. Megan Hicks and Kim Park had to hold her back. The ref blew her whistle frantically, trying to restore order as the crowd fell silent, wondering what in the world had happened.

Coach McKean was furious. "Sit down, both of you!" she hissed. "Tucker, Moran, you're in." As play resumed with two sixth graders in the lineup, she turned to Jamie and Michaela, her jaw set. "I don't know what's going on between you two," she said, "but I've got a team to run. If you can't play as teammates, you can both ride the bench. Now what's it going to take, and how long do you want to sit there?"

She turned her attention back to the game, which was now tied at 7–7, and left the two girls to consider what she'd said.

Jamie looked at Michaela. Michaela looked back at her.

"Well, I don't want to sit here, do you?" she asked.

Jamie shook her head. "We can settle this later," she said.

Michaela nodded. "Coach?" she called. "We're ready to go back in."

The coach gave them a doubtful look. "You sure?" she asked.

"We're sure," Jamie said.

"Let me see you shake on it," Coach McKean demanded.

Jamie took Michaela's outstretched hand and shook it once. It killed her to do it, but sitting on the bench was even worse.

"Okay, get back in there and play like teammates! Time out, ref — substitution!"

Jamie walked back onto the court. The anger

inside her had settled down, and she was able to concentrate and play her game. Michaela, too, devoted her energies to winning, and soon the Sharks had prevailed, 15–11.

Closer than it should have been, Jamie told herself. *Thanks to Michaela, the ball hog.*

As the crowd dispersed, Jamie looked around for her and saw her by the bleachers, pouring her heart out to Jeff. He looked up, staring right at Jamie with a pained, confused look on his face.

Jamie wheeled around and ran back into the locker room. That look of Jeff's hurt worse than anything else. Michaela had stolen his heart — and for that, Jamie was not about to forgive her.

13

Jamie took the long way home, walking by herself through the darkening streets. She wanted to be prepared when she came through the front door.

At least they weren't all lined up on the couch, staring at her as she came in. Jamie heard her dad and Tracy in the kitchen, getting dinner ready. She went up to the swinging door and listened.

"You've got to talk to Jamie, Chuck," Tracy was saying. "She's totally out of control, and there's no use in me talking to her. She sees Michaela and me as the problem. Besides, you're her father — I'm not her mother. It's got to be you."

"I know, Tracy," Jamie heard her dad say, his voice heavy with sadness. "I'm sorry I've waited this long. I just thought that maybe, given time and if we all cut her some slack, Jamie would come around." He let out a deep sigh. "If only she weren't taking it all so badly."

Jamie felt her lip trembling. She *hated* being the "bad one." Hated it with a passion. She went over to the couch and dropped her book bag onto the floor so that they'd know she was home. If there was going to be another "little talk," she might as well get it over with right now.

Her dad pushed open the door and stood there staring at her, his face etched with compassion. From inside the kitchen, Jamie heard Tracy clattering around, taking her frustration out on the dishes as she set the table.

"Could I just say something first?" Jamie asked as he came over to her and opened his mouth to speak.

"All right," he said.

"I just want you to know," Jamie began, talking slowly so she'd get it just right, "that Michaela isn't exactly a little angel. She's purposely trying to get me upset."

"She seems to be succeeding," her dad said.

"You should have seen her push her way onto the volleyball team, Dad!" Jamie blurted the words out in a rush, desperately trying to make him understand.

His eyes remained steady, his expression set. "Jamie, stop it. Listen to me now. I want you to look at *your own* behavior."

"But she —"

"*Your own,* Jamie. You. Just you. Not Michaela. Whatever she's done wrong is her problem, not yours. I want you to take responsibility for yourself." He had her by the shoulders now and was forcing her to look at him. "Understand?"

She nodded slowly, her eyes brimming with tears.

"Good," he said. "Now, ever since Tracy and Michaela got here, you've been treating them like enemies. I don't know what makes you think you can do that. I happen to love Tracy, and Michaela, too. They're just as much my family now as you and Donna."

He paused for a moment to let his words sink in. They did. Jamie could barely breathe. The sobs were choking her. Tears dripped onto her sneakers.

"Look," her dad said, softening a little, "I know I put you in a difficult situation. That's why I've tried to be tolerant up to now. But your behavior's way over the line, Jamie. It's got to stop right now, understand? No matter what you think Michaela's done to you, you've got to forgive her and work to get along with her from now on. If you think about it, I'm sure she's got a lot to forgive *you* for, too, am I right?"

Jamie nodded, unable to speak.

"All right," he said, giving her a hug. "Can I count on you?"

"Y-yes, Dad," she managed to get out.

"Good. I'll see you at dinner in about fifteen minutes." He left her there, disappearing through the swinging door.

Jamie sat there for a minute or two, trying to regain her composure. She went to the downstairs bathroom and washed her face. Then she headed upstairs.

At the top of the stairs, she heard voices behind Donna and Michaela's door. The two of them were talking in hushed tones, like conspirators. Probably thinking up some new way to get her back, Jamie guessed.

She flashed back to the way Michaela had hogged the ball that afternoon, the way she'd flirted with Jeff Gates, wormed her way onto the Sharks, the way she'd offhandedly taken down Jamie's posters and replaced them with her own, as if it had been her room, not Jamie's.

Michaela's a schemer, and nobody realizes it but me, she thought. Still, her dad had made her promise to make up with Michaela. Like it or not, she knew she had to do it — and the sooner she started trying, the better.

With a quick knock, she opened the door a little and said, "Hi, it's me."

"No! Get out!" Donna shrieked, throwing herself against the door so that it shut in Jamie's face. "You can't come in!" she added, holding the door closed with all her weight.

"Fine. Be like that," Jamie said, her resentment coming back in full force. She kicked the door hard, three times, then went across to her own room, slamming the door behind her.

She expected to hear her dad's and Tracy's footsteps pounding up the stairs to see what new disaster had happened. But after a few seconds, when she heard nothing, Jamie relaxed a little.

Looking around the room now, she noticed that something was different. Everything looked pretty much the same as usual, but not quite. *What was it?*

With a sudden shock, she realized that things were not quite where she'd put them. Two of her drawers were slightly open, and she knew she never left them that way. The papers on her shelves were neater than usual.

Panicked, Jamie hurried to her top drawer to look for the leather packet of photos. It was missing!

Someone had been going through her room, her treasures! And Jamie had no doubt who it was.

Stifling a scream of fury, Jamie stormed back across the hall and threw open the door of Donna and Michaela's room.

There they were, on the floor, with Jamie's photos spread all around them! She'd caught them red-handed!

"What are you doing with my stuff?!" she shouted. "Who told you you could go in my room and just take it?"

Donna had been trying to gather everything up and hide it under a large piece of poster board. "Why didn't you knock?!" she screamed back. "You ruined everything!"

"*I* ruined everything? *I* did?" Jamie gasped. Then she pointed to Michaela. "*She's* the one who ruined everything! Until she came along, my life was fine. Now it's totally wrecked!"

Donna stared at her, speechless, those big blue eyes of hers filling with tears.

Michaela's lip was trembling. She covered her mouth with her hand and ran sobbing from the room. Jamie heard her running down the stairs.

There, Jamie thought. She had come right out with the truth. Her dad was totally going to kill her, she knew. And none of them would ever, ever forgive her. But this time, Jamie had no regrets. She had done what she had to do. Michaela was the one who had gone over the line this time, not her.

But as she looked at her little sister, Jamie felt Donna's gaze burning a hole right through her anger.

"You stupid jerk!" she hissed at Jamie. "All we were doing was making you a collage for your birthday!"

Jamie was stunned. "W-what?" she whispered, uncomprehending.

"We were putting together a big display of your whole life," Donna said. "It was Michaela's idea. She wanted to do something to make you like her. That's all she's been trying to do ever since she got here.

107

And you've been so mean to her. Now she's broken-hearted and it's all your fault! I hate you! I hate you, hate you, hate you!"

With that, Donna ran right past her, out the door, and down the stairs to join Michaela.

Jamie stood there alone, her head buzzing, her heart pounding, with the treasures of her life scattered on the floor around her.

14

She'd messed up totally. She looked now at the collage Michaela and Donna had been making. On the poster board were some of Jamie's favorite pictures, including the one of her and her mom taken just before Mom got sick.

Among the pictures were quotes cut out of magazines, things like: "There's no stopping her now!" and "Who's that girl?" and "Viva Volleyball!" which was stuck under a picture of Jamie in her Sharks uniform, spiking the ball at a helpless opponent.

Jamie had to laugh through her tears at that one, and at the headline that warned "Shark Attack!"

All the images on the poster board, all the words, came together perfectly to sum up her life. At the bottom, right in the center, was an empty space for a final photo. Under it was a cut-out quote that said

"Happy Family." Jamie wondered which photo would have gone there. Oh, well. She'd probably never know now.

She had accused Donna and Michaela of stealing her stuff, when all they'd wanted to do was to give her a beautiful gift for her birthday. What Jamie couldn't figure out was *why*. Why had they chosen to do something so nice for her when she'd been so mean to them — to Michaela in particular?

Jamie knew they'd been mad at her — they'd had good reason to be — so why had they decided to give her something so special?

Puzzled, Jamie sat down on Michaela's bed. She put her hand on the pillow and, to her surprise, felt something hard and lumpy underneath. *What's this?* she wondered, reaching under and pulling out a cloth pouch filled with . . .

Photographs! A faded picture of Michaela as a little girl, standing next to a tall, handsome, impish-looking man. . . .

"Her father . . ." Jamie breathed.

For some reason, the fact that Michaela had lost her father around the same time Jamie had lost her

110

mother had never really sunk in. But seeing this photograph, the obvious resemblance between father and daughter, brought it home for her as words never had. She held up another photo, of Tracy, Michaela, and Michaela's father — the whole happy family standing on what looked like a ferry, with the Statue of Liberty in the background.

"She's just like me," Jamie whispered.

Suddenly, Jamie saw herself in Michaela's place. What if it had been Jamie who had had to adjust to a new home, a new school, and a new parent? How would she have acted — and what would she have done if Michaela had treated her as Jamie had been treating Michaela, like the enemy? Jamie closed her eyes, deeply ashamed of herself.

Why hadn't it occurred to her before that she and Michaela had something so deep in common? It was incredible — both of them with their treasured photos, their one link with their deceased parents, both of them struggling to adjust to their new lives.

Jamie had a vision of Michaela discovering *her* photographs, looking through them one by one.

Would she have seen the similarities between Jamie's mom and Jamie? Jamie hoped so.

No wonder Michaela had decided to make the collage. It was her way of saying, "We have so much in common. Why can't we be friends, and sisters?" For Jamie had no doubt that Donna was telling the truth when she said the collage had been Michaela's idea. Donna would never have given Jamie a birthday present when she was mad at her, nor would she have thought of something so original.

Jamie swallowed, trying to get rid of the lump in her throat.

She had misjudged Michaela. She knew now that what everyone had been telling her all along was true — it wasn't Michaela who'd been ruining her life. Jamie had been doing that all by herself, by putting up a wall between her and her new sister!

Well, it was time for that wall to come tumbling down. Jamie sprang to her feet. She carefully put Michaela's photos back into their pouch and replaced it where she'd found it. With one last glance at the poster of her past, Jamie went back to her room, determined to change her future, starting that very moment.

✿　　✿　　✿

Jamie didn't fall asleep until two o'clock in the morning. From the moment she discovered the pouch full of photos under Michaela's pillow, she saw no one (she skipped dinner, not even feeling hungry), and by the time sleep finally overcame her, she had the beginnings of a plan.

The next morning, she was up early, before anyone else, and left the house quickly, her mouth stuffed with a doughnut. Now she was hungry!

She ran all the way to the Gates house. Laurie answered the door in her pajamas. "Whoa!" she said, rubbing her eyes sleepily. "You're up early today. What's up?"

"Come on in the kitchen, I'll tell you," Jamie said. There, over bagels and cream cheese, she told Laurie everything that had happened.

"I told you she was a great person!" Laurie exclaimed. "Oh, I'm so relieved you're finally over it! It's been impossible to talk to you lately."

"I know, I know. I'm sorry. Mmm. These are good. Got any more cream cheese?"

"Here," Laurie offered. "Want some juice with that?"

"Mmph." Jamie nodded affirmatively. Swallowing another mouthful of bagel, she said, "I want to throw Michaela a surprise party, to welcome her to town, okay?"

"Sounds great!" Laurie agreed.

"So here's what we do. We get Coach to call a big pep rally on Thursday, supposedly because we're playing West Side the next day, right?"

"Uh-huh . . ."

"And then when Michaela runs in, we all yell 'Surprise,' and unroll the signs, and stuff like that — and we need a big cake, of course, and the whole school will be there!"

"Cool! I can't wait!" Laurie enthused. "Hey, Sam, Jeff, listen to this!"

Samantha and Jeff Gates had come into the kitchen. Still not able to face anybody, especially Jeff, Jamie concentrated on her food while Laurie told them all about her plan.

"Huh!" Jeff said, smiling his cute crooked grin. "Hey, Jamie, what's up with this? I thought you hated Michaela."

"I did, kind of," Jamie admitted. "I was being a jerk, okay? I'm over it now. End of story."

"Hey, cool with me." He shrugged. "Whatever. This is going to be great. Count me in!"

"Me, too!" said Samantha. "Does Donna know yet?"

"No, and I'm not going to tell her, because she hates my guts and isn't speaking to me," Jamie said.

"No prob," Samantha said. "*I'll* tell her."

"Make sure she doesn't open her big mouth and tell Michaela," Jamie said. She smiled at the thought of Donna straining against all her instincts to keep the secret.

"Don't worry about it," Samantha assured her. "I'll make her promise not to."

"So it's for Thursday night?" Jeff asked.

"Yup," Jamie answered. "That is, if Coach says it's okay."

"Are you kidding?" Laurie asked. "She's dying for you two to make friends! She'll be thrilled!"

"You'll ask her?" Jamie begged.

"Leave it to me," Laurie said.

"I'll make sure the signs get made right," Jeff volunteered. "And I'll ask Michaela to come with me to the pep rally. That way we can be sure she gets there after everyone else is ready."

"Okay," Jamie said, feeling happier than she'd felt in weeks. "This is good. This is super. Well, I'd better get going. I've got a whole lot of work to do. This is one party Michaela's never going to forget!"

Before leaving the house, Jamie took all the money she'd been saving and stuffed it in her wallet. She was going to need a lot, she figured, to cover all she was going to buy.

Her first stop was the poster shop. Here she spent the next hour and a half looking through bin after bin of rolled-up posters, searching for exact matches for the ones she'd torn. She found four of the six, which, considering how old some of Michaela's posters were, was pretty good.

The other two, Jamie decided, would have to be substituted for. She found one of Peppermill, although it wasn't the same one Michaela had had. This one showed the band live, on tour. Jamie thought it was even better than the one it was replacing.

As for the antique Woodstock poster, Jamie knew there was no way to replace it. So she decided to ask the guy at the store about it.

"Oh, yeah, those go for lots of money if they're in good condition," he said. "You got one?"

"Not anymore," Jamie said, frowning. Had Michaela's been in good condition? She tried to remember. It seemed to Jamie that the poster had had a rip in the bottom left corner, but she wasn't sure. At any rate, there was no way she could order another one with the amount of money she had.

Jamie sighed sadly. It hit her that in some ways what she had done could never be undone. She'd have to repay Michaela in spirit, not money.

"What could I get for less that would be sort of the same?" she asked the guy.

"Well, we have some of the Beatles from back then, and the Stones, and Bob Dylan. Do you like any of those?"

"I don't know," Jamie said. "It's for a friend. I guess everybody likes the Beatles, though, right? Let me see that one."

"I've got a bunch of different ones," he told her. "Follow me."

Jamie wound up picking a colorful poster from the *Sgt. Pepper* album. She'd noticed that Michaela had that CD. It wasn't her Woodstock poster, but it would have to do. It was not rolled up like the others but mounted with a cardboard backing and covered with plastic. "How much?" she asked.

When the man told her, she gasped.

"Hey, that's what these things cost," the man said with a shrug. "The Woodstock one costs much more, if you can even get it."

"How much altogether?" Jamie asked, nervously fingering her wad of bills.

Her first purchase took two-thirds of her money. But there was no way she could not get the posters — they were a payback, not a gift, and that had to come first and foremost.

Next stop was the dollar store. Here, Jamie bought a half-dozen small frames for photos. She smiled at the thought of going through Michaela's pouch again, picking out just the right ones to frame.

She made it to the jewelry store with a few bills left in her pocket. Weeks ago, she'd strolled by the store window and stared longingly at the sports pendants. Softballs, basketballs, soccer balls, on gold chains. She'd even mentioned to her dad that she'd like to have a volleyball pendant for her birthday. He hadn't seemed to pay much attention at the time.

Probably thinking about Tracy and asking her to marry him, Jamie thought. *Oh, well.*

"Can you make up a volleyball pendant?" she asked the woman inside the shop.

"Sure, we make those ourselves," the woman answered with a pleasant smile. "Of course, it'll take a week or so. . . ."

"A week? No, that's no good — I need it by Thursday!"

"Oh. I see." The woman thought for a moment. "Well, I suppose we could put a rush on it. Would you like real diamonds in the volleyball, or zirconium?"

"Zirconium, I guess," Jamie replied. "Are the ones in the window real diamonds?"

"No, those are zirconium."

"Great. Zirconium, then," Jamie said, relieved. The ones in the window looked real enough to fool her.

Then the woman told her how much the pendant would be.

For the second time that day, Jamie gasped when she heard the price. "Oh! But I don't have that much!"

119

"I see," the woman said, her smile vanishing.

"Um, could I get it with a fake gold chain?"

"Yes, that would lower the price considerably," the woman said.

Jamie heaved a sigh of relief as she handed over the rest of her money. Her shopping mission was successfully completed. Now to head home and get busy on the hard part.

Before going into the house, Jamie peeked through the living room windows. Michaela and Donna were in the living room, playing checkers. Thinking fast, Jamie headed for the garage. There, she stowed her purchases behind some boxes, where no one would find them until she could get them up to her room unnoticed. Then she doubled back and came in through the front door.

"Hi," she said as she passed the two girls.

Michaela froze, staring down at the checkerboard. Making sure Michaela wasn't watching, Donna looked up at Jamie and threw her a quick wink.

Good, Jamie thought. *Samantha's already told her.* Jamie headed up to her room without trying to make any further conversation. As far as she was concerned, the less that was said between now and Thursday night, the better.

She closed the door behind her, sat down at her desk, and took out some of her best stationery. Picking up a pen, she started to write a letter of apology to Michaela. She thought over all that had gone wrong between them, taking responsibility for everything. It was hard to write the words down, because putting them on paper meant she had to face the truth head-on.

But as hard as it was to write it down, it was going to be ten times harder to read her apology out loud, in front of everybody.

Still, no matter how much it hurt, Jamie was determined to do it. It was the only way to really put the past behind her and make a new start.

15

The next few days went by quickly. Jamie was busy making sure everything was being taken care of. There were all the arrangements to be made, people to be invited, and permissions to be acquired. Jamie had to sneak Michaela's photos out of her room so she could frame them. She had to get cardboard backing to mount the posters she'd bought — and she had to clean out her closet to make room for everything that needed to be hidden away.

In addition to all that, Michaela had to be kept in the dark. This was the hardest part, because Michaela was naturally curious — a couple of days ago, Jamie would have called her nosy — and she kept wandering around when Jamie was whispering on the phone. On those occasions, Michaela would give her a nasty look. Jamie figured Michaela thought she was gossiping about her.

Jamie didn't try to explain. It was better that Michaela believed Jamie was still her enemy. That way, Thursday night would come as a total shock to her.

Jamie smiled at the thought. She couldn't wait to see the look on Michaela's face when she found out what Jamie had really been up to.

Her dad and Tracy already knew — once Donna was clued in, it was only a matter of time before she told them — so they left Jamie alone. It was a huge relief to Jamie when her dad gave her a secret smile at dinner.

In fact, Jamie was feeling fantastic. As bad as she'd felt before, she really appreciated walking around happy for a change. It became a huge effort for her to pretend to be grouchy whenever Michaela was around.

By Tuesday afternoon, the posters were up all over school: "SHARKS PEP RALLY THURSDAY NIGHT AT EIGHT — BE THERE OR BE SHARK FOOD!" "COACH MCKEAN WANTS YOU!" with a picture of Molly McKean shouting something. "SHARPEN THE SHARKS' TEETH THURSDAY NIGHT!" and so on. Everybody was talking about the pep rally.

When Thursday evening rolled around, Jamie made sure she got to the gym first by bolting down her dinner and leaving the house at seven sharp.

"The rally doesn't start till eight," Michaela reminded her. "How come you're leaving now?"

Jamie racked her brain for a quick excuse. "I'm meeting Kim Park there. We're going to give a speech to psych up the team."

Michaela's curiosity seemed satisfied. "Oh," she said. "Well, whatever."

"Yeah," Jamie said. *She thinks I'm leaving to avoid going with her,* she realized. Good. The surprise was still intact. Michaela was totally oblivious. It felt great for once to be one step ahead of Michaela, especially since it was something good.

By eight o'clock, the gym was packed solid. The school band played loudly and enthusiastically, if a little off-key. The cheerleaders, led by Tina Macaluso, were already going through their acrobatic chants as students, parents, and teachers filed inside.

On a platform in the center of the gym were chairs for Coach McKean, Principal Cerruti, and a few other teachers. Soon the team members would be standing in a row on a lower platform in front of the main one.

Jamie had inspected everything but the main banner — the one that read "GO SHARKS! BEAT WEST SIDE!" It was draped from a long rope and cleverly folded so that when clothespins on both ends were removed, the lower half would drop down from behind to say "WELCOME TO EAST SIDE, MICHAELA!"

Jamie went to give the sign one last look, but Kim Park waylaid her. "Jamie," she said, grabbing her and dragging her toward the double doors at the front of the gym, "come on. I heard Michaela's outside. Let's go check."

"But I wanted to check on the sign —" Jamie began.

"It's fine; I checked it myself," Kim said quickly. "Come on, we've got to get everybody ready for the surprise!"

When they got to the front doors, Michaela was nowhere to be seen. Jamie looked up at the clock, which said 8:15. As promised, Laurie and Jeff had seen to it that Michaela, who was coming with them, would arrive late.

"I thought you said she was here," Jamie said.

"That's what they told me. . . ." Kim said, looking around.

Just then, Ms. Cerruti stepped to the microphone and started making a speech. Afterward, it would be Coach McKean's turn.

Too late to check the sign now, Jamie realized. The rally had officially started. Oh, well. She guessed she could trust Kim to make sure it was okay.

Jeff and Laurie came in with Michaela just as the principal was finishing her remarks. "And now, I give the stage over to our favorite coach, Molly McKean!"

There was a huge roar from the crowd. It shook the entire gym as the coach stepped to the microphone.

"First of all, I want to thank everyone for coming," she said, stopping as the crowd cheered again. "With this kind of support, we're going to be having an even bigger party soon!"

Again, the house was rocked. The roaring went on for a full two minutes before the coach could get another word out. "Well, I can see there's no point in giving a long speech, so would the members of the Sharks just come on up here? Come on, everyone, let's show 'em how we feel about them!"

The band launched into the school song, the cheerleaders went wild, and the members of the team, all in uniform, of course, ran up to the lower platform and arranged themselves in a line.

The coach introduced the team members one by one. Michaela was right next to Jamie, on her right. Jamie stepped forward and waved when her name was called. Then it was Michaela's turn.

She stepped forward to acknowledge the crowd, but to her surprise, Coach McKean skipped her name and read out the next one. On and on she went, reading off the names until everyone else had been called. Jamie watched Michaela's smile fade as she wondered why she'd been passed over.

Now came the moment Jamie had been living for all week. Coach McKean cleared her throat.

"Last but not least," she said, "I want to introduce somebody to those of you who haven't met her. . . ."

Jamie saw Michaela start to smile again, relieved that she hadn't been forgotten after all.

". . . Someone who comes to us all the way from New York City and who has given our team a lift while Laurie Gates recovers from her injury — Michaela Gordon!"

As Michaela stepped forward, the clothespins on the sign were pulled, and the bottom half dropped down with its welcome message for her. At that very moment, four girls rolled a square table through the double doors. On the table was a huge cake reading "WELCOME MICHAELA — AND HAPPY BIRTHDAY JAMIE!"

Jamie's jaw dropped. What in the world was going on? She turned around to look at the sign, only to find that it, too, read "WELCOME MICHAELA — AND HAPPY BIRTHDAY JAMIE!"

Jamie wheeled around to face Michaela, who seemed equally shocked. "I can't believe this!" Jamie whispered. "This was supposed to be a surprise party for you!"

"What?" Michaela gasped. "But I planned this whole thing for your birthday!"

As both girls stood there dumbfounded, Coach McKean said, "It looks like we succeeded in surprising both of them, folks!"

The band had just finished playing "Willkom-men," the welcome song from the musical *Cabaret*, and now launched into "Happy Birthday."

Michaela stared at Jamie, blinking back tears of joy. "You did this for *me?*" she asked. "But I thought —"

"I changed my mind," Jamie said, laughing and crying at the same time. "I can't believe you planned a surprise for me, too!"

Laurie came over and gave them both a hug, as best she could with her cast still on. "You guys have no idea how hard it was for everybody to keep both surprises secret!" she said. "Just now, Kim told me you were about to check out the sign, Jamie!"

Jamie gave Laurie a squeeze, then turned to hug Michaela. The crowd erupted in an ear-splitting roar as the two girls held each other.

Then Jamie broke it off and went up to the micro-phone. "I have to say something," she shouted into the mike, holding up her hands for quiet. It took a long time, and she had to repeat it two or three times, but finally the crowd quieted down and the drums stopped thumping.

"I want to thank you all so much," Jamie began. "And especially you, Michaela, for remembering my birthday." She cleared her throat to keep from choking up, then continued. "I wrote something for tonight, something I really need to say, and I want all of you to hear it."

As she fished out her note and wiped the tears from her eyes so she could read it, she saw her dad, with Tracy and Donna, framed in the double doors at the front of the gym.

Jamie smiled. All week, she'd thought she was putting one over on Michaela, while Michaela was doing the same to her. But Donna, her dad, and Tracy had known all along about both plans. What an acting job they'd done!

Jamie held her note up to the light and in a shaky voice began to read it. "Dear Michaela," she said, "this isn't easy for me to say, but I'm sorry for the rotten way I've treated you. From the moment you got here, I never gave you a chance. I didn't want you here, and I made your life miserable on purpose. I thought having you for a sister would ruin my life, but I was wrong. I've come to find out that we have a lot in common. So I hope you'll forgive me.

And I promise that from now on, you can count on me to act like a true sister, and a friend."

She folded up the letter and looked over at Michaela.

Michaela just nodded silently, and the two girls embraced again.

16

By the time they got home, the whole family fell into bed exhausted. The next morning, after the grown-ups left for work and Donna was safely aboard her school bus, Jamie and Michaela walked to school together. They talked the whole way, finally getting to know each other.

"I can't believe you like that song, too!" Michaela said when Jamie started humming it.

"Oh, yeah, I have the CD," Jamie said.

"Me, too! Do you like their latest song?"

"Uck, no."

"Me neither!"

By the time they'd gone the six blocks, they'd found out half a dozen more things they had in common. They parted at the school entrance, off to their separate classrooms. Jamie watched Michaela go. A secret smile crept across her lips. There were still a couple of surprises up her sleeve.

But first, there was the big game. If they lost, it would be the last game Jamie would ever play as a Shark. The season would be over, and next year she'd be in high school. On the other hand, if they won, it could be the beginning of a monthlong play-off season.

Jamie had dreamed of making the play-offs ever since last year, when they'd fallen one game short of the division championship. Now it was within their grasp. All they had to do was beat their arch rivals — the West Side Gophers.

As Jamie went down the hall toward her first-period class, she noticed a poster on the wall, right next to the big one that read "GO SHARKS! BEAT WEST SIDE!"

This poster said "HALLOWEEN DANCE NEXT FRIDAY NIGHT."

"Hi, Jamie," came a familiar voice behind her.

Jamie's heart did a quick flip-flop. She wheeled around, and there was Jeff Gates, smiling at her.

"Hi yourself," she said, darting a quick smile at him before looking away. Had he seen her looking at the sign? Did he know she'd been thinking of him at that very moment? If he did, she'd just melt away and disappear.

"I thought what you did last night was fantastic," he said.

"Oh. Thanks," Jamie said. "It was nothing. . . ."

"No, it wasn't. That was really big of you." He put a hand on her shoulder. "I knew all along you'd come through in the end."

Jamie gulped. "You did?"

"Sure. I kept telling Michaela to give you a little time and you'd come around."

Jamie nodded, looking away, feeling his hand there on her shoulder.

"Um, listen," he went on, suddenly sounding tentative. "If you're not already going with somebody, do you want to go to the Halloween dance?"

"With you?" Jamie blurted out, flabbergasted.

"Uh, yeah," he said, biting his lip. "I mean, you don't have to if you —"

"Oh, no, I do! I mean, I will — I mean, sure!" Jamie said, her legs feeling a little rubbery. "I mean, what about Michaela?"

Jeff blinked. "What about Michaela? She's going with Kevin Hicks."

"Megan's brother?" Jamie asked.

"Yeah. Apparently he likes her, and vice versa. So, do you want to go?"

"Um, yeah, sure!" Jamie said.

"Great. Well . . . I'd better get to class," Jeff said. "See you at the game, huh?"

"Yeah. See you there." Jamie waved as he backed away. She still couldn't believe it — *Jeff Gates had asked her out!*

Four o'clock took forever to arrive. Finally, the Sharks made their way onto the court, doing warm-up stretches as they went. Across the net from them stood the West Side Gophers, in their red-and-gold uniforms.

They seemed confident, Jamie thought. *Too* confident. Well, they were about to be tested as they hadn't been all year. Even in the locker room, Jamie had felt the electricity. The Sharks were ready — ready to take their game to a whole new level.

Outside, it was raining hard. The sound of the rain

on the metal roof of the gym was deafening. Coach McKean had to shout to make herself heard in the pregame huddle.

"Sharks! This is our moment — play your game and you'll never forget this night. Put your hands in here now." They all put their hands together. "We're a family. Let's play like it!"

"GO SHARKS!!" the whole team yelled. The ref's whistle blew. The game was on.

The Gophers had three really tall girls in the front line at the start of the match. The one opposite Jamie was at least six feet. Jamie crouched low. What she lacked in height, she was going to have to make up in leaping ability and sheer determination.

Michaela stood on Jamie's left. At least she was as tall as her opposite number. On Jamie's right, Megan Hicks gave away at least four inches to the girl facing her.

If you just looked at height, it appeared to be a mismatch. No wonder the Gophers seemed so confident of winning. With Laurie Gates, the Sharks' tallest player, injured and unable to play, they probably thought this was going to be a walkover.

Height isn't everything, Jamie told herself as Keisha served and the match began.

The Sharks were on fire right off the bat. Jamie could see the Gophers glancing at each other, fear creeping into their eyes as they realized this was not going to be an easy victory. By the time the Gophers got the serve, it was 6–0, Sharks. The rain pounding on the roof got heavier. Joined with the cheers of the frenzied crowd, the banging of the bass drum and the blaring of horns, it was enough to shake up even a team like the Gophers. They called a quick time-out to try and break the momentum. But the noise just got louder all around them. The band played the theme from *Jaws* faster and faster.

But the Gophers were no pushovers. They had not accumulated so many wins by being easily rattled. They came back strong, using their height advantage to crawl back into the match, finally tying the game at 13–13.

Jamie knew that the next two points would be crucial. Whoever won the first game would have a tremendous advantage. It was now or never. Time to shine.

The Gophers were serving. Jamie, in the front line again, took the pass from the receiver and set Michaela up perfectly. Michaela leaped high into the air, her long arm windmilling so fast it was a blur, and sent the ball smashing into the midst of the hapless defenders.

"Yes!" Michaela cried as Jamie gave her double high fives. Jamie knew that a week ago, she would have tried to spike that ball herself instead of passing to Michaela. She'd matured, and she'd helped her team in the process.

Now it was time for Jamie to serve. She overhanded it, sending a hard slam into the far left corner. The defender, unable to handle it, let it fall, hoping it would land out of bounds long. But the shot hit the tape, right in the corner of the court! It was 14–13, Sharks.

Jamie took the ball to serve for the game. She blew out several deep breaths.

Then she saw a flash of light. Lightning outside. Jamie leaped into the air and hit the ball just as the inevitable thunder clapped.

Everyone in the gym yelled at once. The noise obviously threw the Gophers off guard, because they reacted a split second late. Jamie's serve was aimed right at the center of their back line, but three Gopher players converged on it. None hit it square, and the ball skittered away, hitting the ground.

Game, Sharks!

"No fair!" one of the Gophers complained to the referee. "The thunder distracted us!"

"Game over!" the ref responded. "Can't help the weather."

The Gophers were furious now, and Jamie thought she detected a hint of frustration creeping into their expressions as they took the court for game two.

Good. If they were frustrated, they were in big trouble. *Sharks have killer instinct,* Jamie told herself.

"Let's goooo!!" she screamed to her teammates, leading them onto the floor.

In the second game, Michaela overpowered the Gophers with several hard spikes, and the Sharks took a 7–1 lead with a 5–0 run. And no sooner did the Gophers get the ball back than Michaela robbed them of it again.

"Hey, that's my sister!" Jamie shouted with a big

grin after Michaela dove for the ball and made an almost impossible shot to win back the serve. "I taught her everything she knows!"

Michaela laughed as she took the ball from Jamie and went to serve. "You're sure it's my turn, now?" she asked jokingly.

"Do your thing, girl," Jamie told her.

Michaela hit a hard serve that began another five-point run for the Sharks. The thunder had faded now, but the Sharks were still raining winners on the hapless Gophers, who now looked totally demoralized. They called a time-out, down 12–4.

"Don't let up now, Sharks," Coach McKean urged them. "We've got to put them away!"

The Gophers staged a rally, taking the next three points. But once the Sharks got the serve back, there was no stopping them. It was Jamie serving again now — serving for the match, the division title, the trip to the play-offs. For *everything*.

She could feel the power surging through her, tired as she was. There was an extra something behind her serves, making the Gophers scramble to recover, making it easy for Michaela to smash a pair of devastating winners.

On the final point, the fans stood up, yelling at the top of their lungs, stomping on the bleachers. Jamie served, and once again, Michaela was set up to spike the return.

This time, though, the defender was ready, and she had help. Two Gophers rose to block the spike, sending it screaming back at Jamie!

Jamie dove, her arms outstretched. She saved the ball, then hit the floor hard, chin first. She saw stars, and the room seemed to spin around for a moment. Then her vision returned to normal, and she saw all her teammates standing over her. And when they saw that she was okay, they broke into big smiles.

"We did it!" Kim Park screamed. "We won! We're in the play-offs!"

Jamie rose to her feet, still a little dazed, supported by the arms of her teammates.

"Michaela hit the big winner!" Megan Hicks told her.

"You saved the day, Bonner!" Coach McKean said. "You get the game ball!"

Jamie took it, and suddenly she was overcome with emotion. "No," she said, "this ball is for

Michaela. She's the one who brought us together. Without her, we would never had made it."

She held the ball out to Michaela, who took it, her eyes welling up with tears. "It's ours," she told Jamie. "Ours."

The gym went wild. The Sharks shook hands with the disconsolate Gophers, who would be going home and sitting out the play-offs.

For the East Side Middle School Sharks, the real volleyball season was about to begin.

17

The ride home was like a dream, all of them in the minivan together, one big happy family celebrating a family triumph.

Before leaving the locker room, the team had agreed to get together Saturday night for a celebration at the local ice-cream parlor. They'd gone their separate ways in the rainy parking lot, each of them walking on air. This had been a victory they'd never forget.

But Jamie's mind was on other things. She still had a couple of surprises up her sleeve, and it was almost time to spring them on Michaela.

When they got home, she ran upstairs to her room. She wanted to make sure everything was just as she'd left it that morning. You never knew.

When she was satisfied no one had tampered

with her work, she opened the door and called, "Michaela, could you come up here for a minute?"

"Coming!" came the voice from downstairs. Michaela bounded up the steps with a big smile on her face. "What's up?" she asked.

"Come on in here," Jamie said.

"Okay," Michaela said, passing Jamie and going into the bedroom. Then she stopped dead, gasping in surprise.

"My stuff!" she said, staring in wonder at what Jamie had done.

Michaela's posters lined the walls, each of them beautifully mounted. On the shelf were her trophies, alongside Jamie's — more than a dozen between them, including the volleyball from today's match, signed by the whole team and Coach McKean.

The dresser top was lined with Michaela's treasured photos, displayed in beautiful frames. Everywhere she looked, Michaela couldn't believe what she saw.

"Welcome to your room," Jamie said. "I mean *our* room. I mean, I'd like it if you'd come back," Jamie said, looking Michaela in the eyes. "If you want to, that is."

"Sure, but . . . what about Donna?" Michaela asked. "Won't she be upset?"

Jamie shrugged, "She's young. She'll get over it," she said. "Besides, we'll both be very, very nice to her. In my case, that's a big change, believe me."

Michaela smiled and nodded. "She's a great kid," she said. "You're lucky."

"You mean *we're* lucky," Jamie corrected her. "Oh, wait, there's something else."

"Something else?"

Jamie went to the desk and picked up the little gift-wrapped box. "For my new sister."

Michaela gulped. "Thanks," she whispered, opening the box. "Oh, my —" She held up the volleyball pendant and stared at Jamie incredulously. "You got me this?"

"Uh-huh."

"When?"

"After I acted like such a jerk over that collage you were making me."

"Oh! That reminds me!" Michaela said. "Wait a second. Waitwaitwait. . . ." She hurried across the hall into Donna's room and then emerged carrying a large picture frame. "Here! This is from me and Donna. Happy birthday."

Jamie took the frame and turned it to face her. There was the finished collage of her life, in all its triumphs and tragedies. It took Jamie's breath away. At the bottom, where the caption said "Happy Family," there was a drawing of the five of them, clearly done by Donna. It made Jamie want to weep.

"You didn't leave anyplace on the wall for it," Michaela said. "But you know what? I could rotate a couple of these posters every once in a while. . . . Yeah, let me take down this one."

She reached up and took one down. "Here, give me that," she said. Taking the framed collage from Jamie, she hung it in the poster's place. "There. I think it looks good there. How about you?"

"I think it's perfect," Jamie said, hugging Michaela hard. "Welcome to the family, sis."

Just then, Donna appeared in the doorway. "Hey!" she said, her blue eyes opening wide with surprise. "Can I join in, too?"

"Sure," Jamie said. "We'll make a sandwich!"

"Yay!" Donna said, slamming into both of them with her arms outstretched.

As they all hugged, Jamie looked up to see her dad and Tracy beaming at the scene from the hallway. "Come on in!" she called to them.

"Yeah," Donna chimed in. "Can't make a sandwich without the lettuce and tomato!"

They all shared a laugh. *We really are a big, happy family,* Jamie thought, amazed that it was true.

"Happy birthday, Jamie," her dad said, beaming. "Tracy and I got you this." He handed her a little box. Even before Jamie opened it, she knew what it was.

"A volleyball pendant!" she cried. "Just like yours, Michaela."

"You mentioned that you wanted one," her dad reminded her. "I guess now you're a matching set!"

"You know," Jamie told them all as she fastened her pendant around her neck, "I guess I've learned something really important from all this."

"What's that, pumpkin?" her dad asked, his arm around her shoulders.

Jamie's look took them all in. "I've learned that when life takes a tough shot at you, you've got to jump up and spike it!"

Read them all!

All available in paperback from Little, Brown and Company

Matt Christopher

Sports Bio Bookshelf

Andre Agassi

John Elway

Wayne Gretzky

Ken Griffey Jr.

Mia Hamm

Grant Hill

Randy Johnson

Michael Jordan

Lisa Leslie

Tara Lipinski

Greg Maddux

Hakeem Olajuwon

Emmitt Smith

Mo Vaughn

Tiger Woods

Steve Young

Join the Matt Christopher Fan Club!

To get your official membership card, the Matt Christopher *Sports Pages,* and a handy bookmark, send a business-size (9 1/2" x 4") self-addressed, stamped envelope and $1.00 (in cash or a check payable to Little, Brown and Company) to:

Matt Christopher Fan Club
c/o Little, Brown and Company
3 Center Plaza
Boston, MA 02108